WITHDRAWN
FOR SALE
PRICE

Please rene
shown on yo

www.hertsd____.g___braries

Renewals and
enquiries:

Textphone for hearing
or speech impaired

date

0300 123 4049

0300 123 4041

Hertfordshire

522 353 40 3

The Ellie's War series:

ELLIE'S WAR
Where Poppies Grow

EMILY SHARRATT

SCHOLASTIC

Scholastic Children's Books
An imprint of Scholastic Ltd
Euston House, 24 Eversholt Street, London, NW1 1DB, UK
Registered office: Westfield Road, Southam, Warwickshire, CV47 0RA
SCHOLASTIC and associated logos are trademarks and/or
registered trademarks of Scholastic Inc.

First published in the UK by Scholastic Ltd, 2015

Text copyright © Scholastic Ltd, 2015

ISBN 978 1407 14498 6

A CIP catalogue record for this book
is available from the British Library.

All rights reserved.
This book is sold subject to the condition that it shall not,
by way of trade or otherwise, be lent, hired out or otherwise circulated in
any form of binding or cover other than that in which it is published. No
part of this publication may be reproduced, stored in a retrieval system,
or transmitted in any form or by any means (electronic, mechanical,
photocopying, recording or otherwise) without prior
written permission of Scholastic Limited.

Printed by CPI Group (UK) Ltd, Croydon, CR0 4YY
Papers used by Scholastic Children's Books are made
from wood grown in sustainable forests.

1 3 5 7 9 10 8 6 4 2

This is a work of fiction. Names, characters, places, incidents
and dialogues are products of the author's imagination or are used
fictitiously. Any resemblance to actual people, living or dead,
events or locales is entirely coincidental.

www.scholastic.co.uk

Many thanks to Emma Young

ONE

OCTOBER, 1916

Ellie's eyes drifted from her reflection in the mirror to the window beside her. She looked at the endless rows of grey slate rooftops and, in the distance, a little sliver of sea beneath a vast, silvery sky. It was early in the day but already the street outside was noisy with voices, motorbuses and bicycle bells. After almost three days, Ellie still wasn't used to how much bigger and busier Brighton was than her own village of Endstone. Even the sea looked different here, though she knew she wasn't really that far along the coast from home.

"Here, let me do it." Aunt Frances's voice was low and gentle as usual, but still made Ellie jump. Frances reached out and took hold of the white cap that Ellie was twisting between her hands. "Oh dear, you've got it all crumpled." She attempted to smooth out the cap before placing it on top of Ellie's head and pinning it into place.

"Do you think it will be all right?" Ellie asked anxiously, watching Frances's slender form in the mirror as she added one last hairpin. "Should I iron it again before we go?"

"It will be fine," Aunt Frances said soothingly, her hands on Ellie's shoulders. "*You* will be fine. But we mustn't be late. Matron doesn't like that at all."

For days, Ellie had felt as though a snake were slowly slithering and writhing in her stomach. It lurched sickeningly at her aunt's words. "Oh, let's go, then," she said, a note of panic creeping into her voice. "I don't want to be in trouble on my first day."

"All right," Frances agreed. "Are you sure you've had enough to eat, though? It's been so busy in the hospital lately that we often don't get to stop for lunch until very late. Or at all, some days."

"I'm sure, thank you," Ellie said tightly. In truth, she had barely managed a slice of the toast Aunt Frances's landlady had set before them in the small kitchen of their digs, and hadn't even been able to look at her boiled egg. With growing food shortages, including bread, it seemed criminal to waste a thing, but she could not have swallowed another mouthful.

Frances looked appraisingly at their reflections in the mirror. Ellie had always looked more like her father's side of the family – with their dark hair, open expressions and narrow but strong frames – than her mother's. In their matching blue dresses, white aprons, and black stockings and shoes, she and Aunt Frances could almost have passed for sisters, especially now that Ellie was nearly as tall as her aunt. Frances smiled, gave Ellie's hand a quick squeeze and then led the way out of the room.

As Ellie hurried behind, trying not to trip in her new shoes, she attempted to calm herself by repeating in her head, over and over, how much she had wanted this, how incredible it was that she was here at all.

Three months ago, when she had first told her family and friends that she wanted to become a volunteer nurse like Aunt Frances, she had never believed that her mother would allow it. But Josephine

Phillips had changed a lot since before the war. Having seen her daughter going first to work at the munitions factory near Endstone and then – most crucially – helping out in the aftermath of the terrible explosion there, trying to keep her tucked away at home seemed more pointless than ever.

Not that Mother had been happy about it. Ellie had still had to fight her case; her mother had been particularly uncomfortable about her move to Brighton. But there was no hospital in Endstone, or any near enough that she could easily travel back and forth from home every day. Besides, no hospital other than Brighton would have taken her. She was officially too young to be a nurse, but somehow her aunt had secured her a position on the wards, and of course a place to stay.

As she followed Aunt Frances out the house into the damp air of the autumn morning, Ellie contemplated how she already felt like a different person from the one who had set off for Brighton three days earlier. There had been so many first experiences. Leaving Endstone properly for the first time ever. Saying goodbye to Mother and little Charlie, and Jack. Jack, her best friend, who had only just come back from war so changed. . . Ellie felt her eyes begin to burn as she thought of Jack seeing her off at the train station. She'd urged him not to, as he still wasn't able to walk long distances after his leg had been injured in the factory explosion, but he had insisted. Thomas Pritchard, Endstone's young doctor, had hung back diplomatically as Jack and Ellie had stared at each other fiercely, and then hugged tightly, as if they were trying to commit the other's touch to memory. Then, when a tear escaped the corner of Jack's eye, he had dashed it off roughly with his sleeve, grumbling, "Go on, get out of here. You're embarrassing old Tom with your soppy displays."

Then there had been the experiences of travelling such a long distance by train on her own, and having to make her way alone from the station to the digs, as Aunt Frances was at work. Living in a house with lots of strangers. . .

And now she was about to face the biggest, most frightening new experience yet. She was going to be working in a busy hospital full of injured veterans, as a volunteer nurse.

"Are you . . . are you *sure* the matron realizes how young I am?" she croaked as Aunt Frances strode purposefully down the street, her heels ringing off the pavement. The streets were getting busier and Ellie had to duck around carts and bicycles and other pedestrians as she scampered to keep up with her aunt. "And she's definitely all right about it?" she added between panted breaths.

Aunt Frances gave her a sympathetic glance as she turned a corner, not slowing her pace. "Of course I'm sure. It is certainly irregular for them to accept a volunteer as young as you, but I explained about your experience helping out in Wesley's surgery, about how it amounts to as much training as many of the professional nurses have had. And of course having two doctors' letters of recommendation helped a great deal."

Ellie managed a weak smile. Young Doctor Pritchard had worked in the Endstone village surgery since before Father went away to war, and Dr Mertens had joined him there after Father died. The doctors were supportive of Ellie's nursing plans – and had been enlisted in the battle to convince both Mother and the matron at Frances's hospital. Ellie felt a fresh wave of gratitude at the thought of the two of them, swamped with the increasing demand at the Endstone surgery, taking the time to write in support of her application. Just picturing them in the familiar building, surrounded by familiar patients and doing familiar work brought on a wave of homesickness. She pushed it back down.

"Ellie, I know it's frightening, and it's perfectly natural to be nervous on your first day, but try not to worry too much," Frances said, maintaining her brisk pace. "We've had so many injured soldiers recently, we're glad of any help we can get. You will be the youngest nurse, it's true, but there have been many volunteers who have arrived with much less experience. Almost everybody is having to learn as they go along and nobody can really keep on top of all that there is to be done. We're just having to do the best we can. Besides, you're a natural nurse; anyone who has seen you care for an unwell person agrees on that. Your father would be so proud if he could see you now."

Ellie knew that part was true, and this time her smile was genuine. When Father had been alive, the idea of her being a nurse hadn't crossed any of their minds, but she was certain he would have approved. And being here, in the city in which he had grown up, preparing to do medical work as he had done, made him feel somehow closer.

Ellie hadn't been to Brighton for such a long time; since her grandparents had died, in fact. Father had always been busy with work, even before he went off to war, and Mother didn't like to be away from home. Ellie had been so young on those last visits; she only had the vaguest memories now: half-recalled smells of seaweed, freshly caught fish and her grandmother's blackcurrant crumble; the feel of the pebbles under her feet as she paddled at the beach; the creak of the leather in her grandfather's favourite armchair as she sat in his lap and listened to him telling stories. The city she moved through now was entirely unfamiliar to her. She couldn't get used to the number of people or the contrast between them: the elegant ladies taking the sea air; the injured soldiers being pushed along the seafront in wheelchairs; the extreme poverty of the beggars who gathered around the train station.

As they walked swiftly down the lightening streets, Frances pointed out various landmarks and sights of local interest that Ellie might not remember from earlier visits. Then, before Ellie knew it, the hospital was looming in front of them.

It was an imposing, somewhat unfriendly looking building, the red bricks darkened by years of exposure to the smoke of the city. Ellie's snake completed a slow, nauseating circuit of her abdomen and she felt her mouth go dry.

Aunt Frances turned to face her. Her smile was still fixed in place but her eyes were anxious. "Ellie, I really don't want you to worry, but I feel I should warn you. . . People do tend to find Matron rather intimidating, at least when they first meet her; there's no two ways about that, I'm afraid. She can be a little . . . brusque; it's just her manner – try not to take it personally. Her bark is much worse than her bite. All right?"

Ellie thought of Mother: her near-constant looks of disapproval; her criticism delivered either subtly or directly; the feeling that nothing Ellie did was ever, ever good enough. She thought of coping without Father; of surviving even when Jack seemed lost to her. She lifted her chin. "I think I'll be fine."

Aunt Frances's smile broke wide open. She lifted her hands to Ellie's shoulders and gave them a tight squeeze. "That's my girl." Then she dropped them again and adopted a businesslike expression. "Come on."

TWO

LATER THAT DAY

As they walked in through the main doors of the hospital, Aunt Frances continued to talk while leading the way:

"I'll take you to meet Matron first of all. She will want to—" She broke off, drowned out by the cacophony in the hall leading to the wards. It reminded Ellie of the scenes outside the factory following the explosion: hurried shouts, screams and moans of pain and fear, the smell of blood and chemicals in the air. . .

"Nurse Phillips, can you assist over here, please?" came a voice. Ellie startled at the sound of her own name, but realized it must be Aunt Frances who was being addressed. "We've had more than fifty new patients in at once from France this morning. . ." A nurse was coming towards them, her apron spattered with blood. "They've been brought more or less direct from the field hospital so many of them haven't had more than the most basic treatment. The base hospitals are overwhelmed, apparently. . ."

Aunt Frances glanced at Ellie but her eyes were darting around. "I'm sorry, Ellie, I have to help. Keep an eye out for Matron, and she or someone else should be able to get you sorted."

Ellie nodded mutely, but her aunt was already moving out of sight before becoming lost in the sea of people. She backed hurriedly into the wall as a trolley-bed was wheeled in front of her. It took her a moment to identify what she was looking at; at first glance the man on the stretcher just seemed a mess of blood soaking through his blue pyjamas. The sound escaping him was barely human.

"Nurse Barker," came a call from a different direction. "We're taking those that can walk upstairs."

Another nurse, holding the elbow of a soldier who was hobbling along on crutches, his eyes bandaged, replied with a cheerful, "Righty-oh," which seemed to Ellie as out of place here as Charlie's giggles always did in church.

Ellie ducked out of the way of another stretcher. She could feel herself growing flushed. She needed to find someone who could tell her what to do; she just felt in the way as it was. But everyone she could see was busy.

"Excuse me," she hazarded to a nurse and doctor, who were spreading a sheet over a stack of boxes – a makeshift bed, Ellie realized with horror; they must be running out.

They looked at her distractedly, and before she could even ask them if they knew where Matron might be, a man was being lifted from a stretcher on to the "bed" accompanied by a stream of information from the doctor:

"He's lost a lot of blood, and the journey hasn't helped matters. I'm not sure we're going to be able to save the leg. . ."

Ellie moved away. Casting wildly around the huge room – she was beginning to feel desperate now – she caught sight of a nurse whose face reminded her of Daisy, with whom she had grown close when working at the factory at home. But as she began to move towards her, the nurse pulled a flimsy curtain around the bed she was standing beside – not before Ellie had glimpsed a soldier being held down by two other nurses, fresh blood pouring from his side to mingle with the dark brown and black stains that covered him.

Ellie squeezed her eyes closed where she stood, fighting the urge to run from the building and back to her digs. With her eyes shut, the sounds around her became deafening, yet also clearer.

"Nurse? Nurse, can you help me, please?" a voice sounded behind her. The accent was from London's East End and, Ellie was relieved to note, the man didn't sound wild with pain like so many of the others.

"Excuse me, Nurse? Could you help me, please?"

Ellie opened her eyes and looked about the room. Nobody else seemed to have heard the man. She didn't hold out much hope of getting someone's attention. She turned around and was startled to see a young soldier sitting up in his bed and staring straight at her.

"Oh!" Her hand went to her chest in a questioning gesture, but she moved towards him all the same.

He grinned sheepishly at her. His head was bandaged, but she could see tufts of sandy-coloured hair poking out from under the white gauze. His right arm was in a sling and held tight to his chest.

"I'm very sorry, Nurse, I know everyone's really busy. And it's not urgent – I can wait until you've helped the blokes that need it more, of course."

"It's all right," Ellie replied, moving closer still. "What do you need?"

"It's just my bandage, Nurse," the young soldier said, gesturing towards his sling. "It's awful tight. Feel as though it's cutting off the circulation!"

"Oh," Ellie said again. She glanced around once more, but she knew there would be no one else available to help. "Well," she said, her voice getting stronger, "I'm sure I can do something about that."

She reached behind his neck to untie the sling, supporting the arm with one hand before the fabric went slack.

"So, you've just arrived this morning from France?" she asked, as the sling fell away to reveal his arm, which was indeed very tightly bandaged. Ellie could see his fingertips were going white.

"That's right," he said.

"Try to keep this arm very still," Ellie murmured, not wanting to interrupt him. She looked around and spied a cabinet. When she opened it, she saw that it was filled with supplies, including clean bandages. She felt her discomfort falling away, the noise all around her seeming to quiet as she grew focused on the task.

"I think normally more of us would have been treated at the base hospital," the soldier continued, as Ellie returned to his side and began to gently unwind his bandage. "But there were just too many of us. They wanted to get those of us who'd copped Blighties – or worse – home and out of the way."

Ellie unwrapped the last of the bandage, revealing his arm, which was covered with mottled bruises and strapped to a splint. Some deep-looking flesh wounds had been closed up with stitches and dressed in now-discoloured gauze.

The soldier gave a sigh of relief. "That's so much better, thank you, Nurse."

"I'm just going to re-dress these abrasions," Ellie said, "then I can get you bandaged up more comfortably."

16

She worked contentedly. Despite the severity of the soldier's injuries – and those around them – this work was familiar and reassuringly routine for Ellie after all her hours in the Endstone surgery.

She cleaned the superficial wounds carefully, but still the soldier winced and paled at each minute movement of his arm.

"Sorry," she whispered.

"That's all right, Nurse. Has to be done!" the soldier said with forced cheer.

"What are Blighties?" Ellie asked, hoping to distract him.

"Oh," the soldier said, dragging his eyes away from his arm. "A Blighty is a wound bad enough to get you sent home, but not necessarily as bad as. . ." He jerked his head in the direction of the man to his right. This soldier was motionless and silent, his left pyjama leg stitched up at the knee.

Ellie began to wrap the fresh bandage around his arm as slowly and gently as she could. The soldier sucked in a quiet breath but carried on talking. "I'm lucky, I know. Means I get away from that hellhole, if you'll excuse my language, Nurse." Ellie smiled to show him that she wasn't offended. "Might even get to see my family."

"You're married?" Ellie asked, as she pinned the bandage in place.

"I am," the man replied, and this time his smile was huge and unforced. "My Tilly's everything to me. Her and our two little girls."

"How old are they?" Ellie put on a fresh sling and tied it behind his neck again, noticing a little row of bites along his hairline as she did so. Lice.

"They're three, almost four."

"Twins!"

"That's right," he said with a grin. "A proper handful."

"That's the same age as my little brother—" Ellie began, but at that moment a barking voice cut across her, making her jump.

"Who are you and just *what* do you think you're doing?"

Ellie turned, her smile falling from her face. In front of her was a short, scowling woman in a grey dress, with a smart little scarlet cape tied around her neck. Her hair was pulled back so tightly from her face that her skin looked taut, her frowning eyebrows pulling in the opposite direction and creating a tug-of-war across her forehead.

"Matron?" Ellie ventured, her voice emerging as a squeak.

"The question was not who *I* am. I am perfectly well aware of that fact, thank you," the woman boomed. "The question was who on earth *you* are, and what are you doing with my patient."

"I'm Ellie – Eleanor Phillips. Frances Phillips's niece."

"I'm still at a loss as to how that qualifies you to wander in off the street and start tampering with the work of medical professionals."

Matron barely came up to Ellie's nose, but that made her no less fearsome.

"I didn't wander off the street. I'm starting work here today—" Ellie began to protest, at the same time as the soldier piped up:

"It's my fault, Matron, I asked her to do it. And she's been ever so—"

"Silence!" Matron thundered. "Both of you! *Nurse* Phillips, you have not even signed in and completed the necessary paperwork. What on earth possessed you, I do not know—" She raised her hand as Ellie opened her mouth, silencing her once more. "Nor do I wish to. You volunteers are all the same – thinking that a life of idleness is just as good a qualification as the years of training the rest of us have undergone."

Ellie puffed out an angry breath but otherwise stayed quiet.

"Private," the matron continued, "in case there is some confusion, I am in charge of the nursing staff in this hospital, not you. If you wish to take over from me, you will have to apply for my post through the proper channels. Now, Nurse, if you would be so kind as to come with me," Matron continued, her voice acid with sarcasm, "perhaps we might be able to put you to some use."

She turned on her heel and began to stalk off. Ellie risked a quick glance at the young private and instantly regretted it; his expression caused her to clamp her hands to her mouth in an attempt to stifle the bubble of laughter rising up her throat.

She scurried through the maelstrom after Matron, terrified of losing sight of her. As she caught up with the stout older woman, Ellie thought longingly of the impression Jack would have done of her. She tried to commit the details of Matron's tirade – her voice and appearance – to memory so that she could put them in her next letter. Her first day had barely begun and already she had so much to tell him.

THREE

LATE NOVEMBER, A FEW WEEKS IN

Ellie reached the end of the room and leaned her broom against the wall. Then she took the dustpan and brush – the handles of which she had tucked into the waistband of her apron – and crouched to sweep up the pile of dust and debris. Her back twinged as she did so, reminding her of the constant aches she had acquired working in the factory. In fact, she thought, slamming the dustpan against the edge of the bin with unnecessary force, in many ways her work here was similar to what she had done at the factory – dull, repetitive and physically exhausting.

On her first day, after getting Ellie to fill out sheet

after sheet of paper, and spending what felt like hours going over the many rules of the hospital, Matron had allocated her to this ward, where she worked under Ward Sister Phyllis Adam, a nurse who looked to be in her late twenties. Sister Adam seemed to have adopted Matron's fastidious ways, and enforced them – particularly where Ellie was concerned – with great relish.

Aunt Frances worked on a different ward with more critical patients, so Ellie didn't see her from the start of the day until the end – and when they were on opposing shifts, not even then.

On that first day, Matron had made it clear that Ellie's tasks would be limited to cleaning and "correct maintenance of the ward", as well as serving the soldiers' meals. This, she insisted, was appropriate work for the most junior nurse, particularly one who – as she reminded Ellie fiercely – was the youngest volunteer the hospital had ever accepted. But Ellie was convinced that she was being punished for what Matron clearly saw as unpardonable presumption in treating the soldier on her first day. When Ellie had dared to point out that she had a lot of experience in patient care, Matron's response had been unambiguous.

"Yes, Doctors Mertens and Pritchard made that clear in their letters to me. What they didn't mention, but which was equally obvious to me, is that you have been indulged and encouraged to think of yourself as possessed of far greater skill and expertise than is in fact the case. I can assure you that there is no place for such pride here, nor shall it be tolerated. You are extremely fortunate that I accepted you for work at all; I hope you realize that I can just as soon send you home should you prove troublesome."

"Yes, Matron," Ellie had replied, through clenched teeth, trying to prise open the tight fists she had formed involuntarily.

Ellie had hoped that if she kept her head down and did as she was told, she might be allowed to take on responsibilities beyond cleaning after the first few days. But more than a month in, there was still no sign of things changing.

Now Ellie finished stacking the clean bedpans on the shelf, having replenished the stores of bandages, clean cloths and other supplies from the trolley.

She checked the fob watch that was attached to the top of her apron. Only five minutes until Matron's next inspection; this meant it was time for her least favourite task.

Sighing, Ellie walked to the first of the six beds on the right-hand side of the room. Smiling apologetically at the soldier who lay there reading the newspaper, she ducked down to the floor beside him.

"Carry on, love," he said cheerfully as she took out her pocket handkerchief, used it to measure the distance between the bed and the wall, and made minute adjustments to get it in line.

She made sure to keep her grumbling internal, feeling Sister Adam watch her beadily as she moved from bed to bed, making sure they were all perfectly aligned.

When she reached the twelfth bed, on the opposite side, she began the circuit again, this time ensuring that all the castors on the legs were facing the same way. Hidden from view as she clambered around on hands and knees beneath the beds, Ellie allowed herself a grimace as she kept up a constant, terse inner monologue:

Oh, yes, because I'm sure it matters hugely to these men – who have seen horrors we can only imagine; lost their limbs or their sight or their memories; been freezing and starving and eaten alive by lice; been away from their homes and their families and their friends – I'm sure they care so very much that the wretched castors on their beds – which they can't even see! – are facing the same way!

As she completed the job on the last bed, the sound of a throat being ostentatiously cleared at the top of the ward caused her to hurry out from beneath it, banging her head in the rush. She straightened her cap, scrabbling to her feet, and saw Sister Adam – flanking Matron with her chin in the air like a pompous lapdog – smirk.

Ellie stood nervously to attention, feeling like a soldier herself, as Matron completed her lap of the ward. No detail escaped her notice, and Sister Adam's own handkerchief was whisked out on more than one occasion, to confirm that the beds were indeed level with one another.

At last Matron reached the end of the room and – with a curt nod which Ellie knew signified it had passed the inspection – swept from the ward without uttering a word. Ellie huffed in relief; she had long since given up hope of a comment of approval.

Sister Adam watched the matron go, her posture rigid, then swung to face Ellie. "Well, Nurse Phillips, you may serve the patients their lunch now."

Ellie nodded mutely, careful as ever not to show the sister how much she relished this task. She felt sure that to do so would result in it being taken from her. Still, she couldn't quite squash a new bounce in her step as she took the trolley of lunch trays that had just been brought up from the kitchen, and pushed it to the first bed.

"Here we are, Private Garrett, I'll bet you're ready for this," she said smilingly to the young soldier, who had been poring over a letter. He had been treated for various infected wounds and damage to his eyes and lungs from chlorine gas. To everyone's relief, he seemed to be recovering, though his eyes were still very red, and his breathing laboured.

"You're not wrong, Nurse!" he wheezed as she unfolded the legs for the tray so that it could stand up over his middle. She longed to stay and talk with him, but could feel Sister Adam's eyes boring into her back, so she smiled again and moved on to the next bed.

"Lunch is here, Corporal," she said gently to the older man. Learning all the military ranks had taken her much of the first couple of weeks but she was always careful now to call every man by the correct title. Before handing him his tray, Ellie helped Corporal Snow to sit up. He had suffered a serious head injury and lay with his eyes closed for most of each day, but he was always impeccably polite.

"Thank you, my dear," he said now, as she plumped the pillows behind his back. "You're very good to me."

"Come along, Nurse Phillips," Sister Adam said sharply behind her. "The other men are hungry too."

Ellie ground her teeth but hurried on. When she reached the furthest bed on the left-hand side of the room, she approached a little more warily. Private Das – the young Indian soldier – was sitting up, turning the pages of his book with his good arm, seemingly as oblivious to her as ever. His other arm was tightly bandaged – the result of a nasty shrapnel wound that had become infected. The eighteen year old had also had a very bad break to his leg, which hadn't been set properly on the battlefield and so had needed to be re-broken and set again once he got to Brighton. As a result, it was taking a long time to heal. This leg stuck out stiffly on top of the bed covers.

Before coming to Brighton, Ellie had never seen anyone of a different-colour skin; indeed, the Mertens family were the first non-English people she had ever spent any time with. Until January of that year, the Royal Pavilion in Brighton had housed one of several hospitals in the city for Indian soldiers who had fought and been injured in the war – and even now that they had closed, there were still many Indian soldiers in Brighton. Ellie knew it was rude to stare, but she found herself mesmerized by the sight of them; her imagination dazzled by the thought of their faraway homes, and their surely very different lives.

Private Das was the only Indian soldier on Ellie's ward and she longed to speak to him, but he showed no such interest. At first she had wondered if he might not speak English, but Grace, another nurse who worked on the ward, had done away with that notion.

"Oh, I thought that at first too. But he does – better English than me, if I'm honest! It's just he doesn't seem to want to chat. Some of them are like that; it's not personal. It's best to leave him be."

None of the men on the ward had known each other beforehand, but little friendships and alliances had been formed after they had lived side by side for so many weeks and months. Private Das seemed very much on the outside of these interactions.

As she took his tray from the trolley and turned to face him, Ellie stared in fascination at his eyelashes – thicker, darker, longer and curlier than any girl's – resting against his cheeks like moth wings as he gazed fixedly down at his book.

"Good afternoon, Private Das," she said shyly.

He put his book to one side to make space for the tray, but didn't respond, didn't even look at her. His face was more like a collection of shifting light and shadow than features that Ellie could pinpoint or describe.

As she propped his tray up, Ellie tried again. "I'm sure you'll be delighted to know that it's potato soup on the menu again today."

This time he slowly lifted his eyes. They were darker than she'd thought possible; she couldn't see where the pupil ended and the iris began. He stared at her for a long moment and she felt her heart rate speed up. Would he finally say something to her?

Slowly, slowly, he looked back down and unfolded his napkin.

Ellie's skin burned as she heard a snort behind her. She turned to face Sister Adam, who said, with a sneer, "Why don't you stop bothering the patients, Nurse Phillips, and get on with your job?"

Ellie moved away from the bed and said tightly, before she could stop herself, "You must be at a loose end yourself, Sister Adam, if you're having to follow the likes of me around."

The sister's nostrils flared. "You seem to be confused about the chain of command on this ward, Phillips," she hissed. "But if you're struggling with even this most basic task perhaps I can take over and you can change the bedpans again instead."

Ellie drew in a deep breath and tried to soften both her expression and her tone. "Thank you, Sister, that won't be necessary. I did the bedpans less than half an hour ago. I will try to be quicker handing out the lunch. I'm sorry."

Private Pope was perched on the end of Private

Brown's bed; the two men were playing draughts. They hadn't known each other before being allocated to the same ward, but had quickly discovered that they were from villages not thirty miles apart in Somerset, and had become firm friends. Both were trying to repress grins at the tense exchange between the two nurses, though Private Brown turned his to a sympathetic grimace when he caught Ellie's eye.

Ellie felt sure her cheeks were scarlet. She hurriedly handed out the rest of the trays without further attempts at conversation with the men, all the pleasure from the job lost.

But as she splashed home through black puddles that evening, holding her umbrella in front of her to prevent the wind from driving the rain into her face, it was not Sister Adam but Private Das she found herself thinking about. Grace was right that not all the men wanted to talk, though usually the ones on Ellie's ward were past the most critical stage and keen for company and conversation. But Private Das's silence seemed different somehow.

Or maybe it was just her own curiosity about him that made it seem so.

She reached the front door of the digs, her feet soaked through in her black loafers, and wrestled with the stiff key in the lock. Despite having to wrangle with it, she felt a thrill at being so grown-up and independent that she had her own key. In Endstone even her mother didn't usually feel the need to carry one; hardly anyone locked their doors there.

Ellie shook her umbrella out in the doorway, then put it in the umbrella stand while pulling the door closed with her other hand.

"Awful evening, isn't it?" remarked the landlady, Mrs Joyce, emerging from the kitchen.

"Horrible," Ellie agreed, taking off her sodden coat and hanging it up.

"There's stew on the stove for you when you're ready," Mrs Joyce continued, "And here's some post."

Ellie looked up eagerly and took the envelope from her hand. "Thank you," she said, feeling a smile spread across her face at the sight of that careful handwriting. "I'll just go and get changed first. . ."

"That's fine, dear." The skin around Mrs Joyce's eyes crinkled. "You take your time reading your letter and help yourself to dinner when you're ready. I'll be knitting in my parlour."

Ellie scampered up the stairs and into the room she shared with Frances. She had to force herself to put the letter down while she clambered out of her wet things and into a comfortable skirt and jumper. Stuffing her feet into her slippers, she collapsed backwards on to her bed and tore the envelope open.

More of Jack's writing, painstakingly neat, stretched across the single sheet. Ellie's eyes devoured it hungrily.

Dearest Ellie,

Well, here I am, writing again, though you know I don't enjoy it. I hope you appreciate my efforts! I wouldn't have troubled myself only I do so look forward to getting your letters and thought you might not send any more if I didn't do my bit and reply.

I'm glad to hear you are settling in well in Brighton and at the hospital, though that Sister Adam and the matron sound like a grim pair. Luckily, I never need to worry about you. I'm sure you are taking no nonsense from anyone. (Maybe the sister has a friend who writes to her saying, "That Nurse Phillips sounds a ferocious beggar! Don't let her bully you!")

It still feels very strange that you're not just across town. I know I was the one who was away last year, but it's different when you're left behind, isn't it?

You'll be glad to hear that I'm building up strength in my leg again nicely and able to get round on it more and more, though it still aches a fair bit if I've done too much.

There's no sign of the factory being reopened, so I'm helping out in the shop a bit. I usually sit behind the counter so Mam and Anna can get on with checking the stock, doing the accounts and the like. I do feel like a bit of a useless lump, though. The sooner I can be out and working properly again, the better!

Thomas reckons I might be strong enough to manage a journey on my own before long, and as soon as he sounds the all-clear, I'll be on the first train to Brighton. Now, you lucky devil, what do you think of that? That should cheer

*you up the next time this Sister Adam is being a
harpy!*

*Take care of yourself and write to me again
soon. A nice long letter, please, I know how you
can rattle them off.*

All my love,

Jack

Ellie's smile was so wide that her jaw was beginning to
ache. Jack would come to see her! Letters were all well
and good, but as he said, Jack didn't enjoy writing
them, and it wasn't anything like sitting next to him,
anyway. They had never been apart for so long in all
their years of friendship – not even when he'd been
away at war – and she couldn't wait to see him.

FOUR

A FORTNIGHT LATER, MID DECEMBER

Ellie finished sweeping the floor and tucked the dustpan back into her waistband. The work was so mindless and repetitive that she sometimes felt as though weeks had passed with nothing but the floor becoming dirty, then clean, then dirty again to mark the time. A sudden sneeze escaped her, and she was scrabbling for her handkerchief before a second one could give Sister Adam the excuse to reprimand her for exposing the patients to infection, when Grace walked in.

"God bless you!" Grace exclaimed as Ellie sneezed again into her handkerchief.

37

"Thank you." Ellie sniffed. "Are you just starting your shift?" she asked, looking into the older girl's smiling face. Grace was a firm favourite with both the patients and the rest of the staff, with her thick, honey-coloured hair, wide eyes and ready laugh.

"I am, so I can take over here. Matron wants to see you."

"Oh?"

Grace burst out laughing, causing a few of the nearby men to look up and smile fondly at her. "No need to look so worried," she said, patting Ellie's shoulder.

"Are you sure about that?"

"Well. . . Well, she didn't seem angry. At least, no more so than usual." Grace laughed again, the sound startlingly loud in the hush of the ward. "Here, let's check you over."

Together the girls inspected every inch of Ellie's uniform, making her cap straight, smoothing her apron, even checking that underneath her fingernails were clean.

"I don't see anything she could complain about," Grace declared at last.

"Hmm," Ellie replied.

"I know, I know, that's never stopped her before. But you'd better hurry or you'll be in trouble for keeping her waiting!"

Ellie let out a yelp and scampered from the ward.

Ellie hadn't been to Matron's office since her first day at the hospital. It was on the ground floor, which meant Ellie had to go down two flights of stairs and pass the critical wards on the way. She had become a lot more accustomed to the horrific battle wounds, and to the sheer volume of men, since her first day. But the contrast with the relative calm on her ward always took her by surprise.

Reaching the door to Matron's office, Ellie gave her apron one last nervous smoothing-down, sucked in a deep breath and knocked. Her mind was still racing through everything she'd done that day, trying to find what might have given Matron cause to reprimand her again. The ward hadn't been inspected yet, so it couldn't be that. She was sure she hadn't forgotten to give any of the men their breakfast. . . Unless it was to do with her visit home at the end of the week.

She'd had two letters earlier in the week telling her

that Mother was unwell again – one from Thomas; one from Mother herself. Thomas had suggested that she might be able to get home for a visit, to give Charlie some attention and to help him persuade Mother to accept more help from the other villagers. Ellie had been unsure how much use she would be, given that she was too frightened even to broach the subject with Matron. In the end she had spoken to Aunt Frances, who had taken matters into her own hands and spoken to Matron. To Ellie's surprise, permission to go home for the weekend had been granted readily. But perhaps now she would see that it was more complicated after all.

"Come in!" Matron's ringing tones carried easily through the heavy door, startling Ellie from her thoughts.

Ellie pushed it open. "You wanted to see me, Matron?"

"Ah, Nurse Phillips, you have deigned to join me. I trust I didn't take you away from any more pressing tasks?"

Ellie's mouth gaped as her brain struggled to come up with an answer that would be acceptable to the fierce woman before her. She was reluctant to suggest that she thought her other work was more important than the obeying the matron's summons. Her mouth snapped shut again, defeated.

"And you do know the hem of your skirt is supposed to be two inches," Matron continued, without waiting for a response. "Do I need to get my tape measure out to confirm that yours is scarcely one?"

"No, Matron, I'm sorry. I will adjust it this evening." Ellie looked down at the bottom of her skirt, and kept her chin tucked in, so that the older woman couldn't see her expression. Had Matron called her all the way down here to complain about her hem, then?

As she looked up again, she saw Matron raise, one heavy brow but the older woman didn't press the matter further. "Nurse Phillips, I am assigning you to assist with changing the patients' dressing on your ward now, in addition to your maintenance tasks, and of course to distributing the meals. Sister Adam has other tasks to attend to and, naturally, Nurse Boyle is not always available. Do you think you can manage it?"

Ellie stared blankly, the words taking a moment

to cut through her circling thoughts of what else she might have done wrong. Her eyes lit on a photograph of a young soldier in uniform on the matron's desk.

"Nurse Phillips, are you even listening to me?" Matron's brows were now furrowed.

"I am, Matron. I beg your pardon. Yes! I mean, yes, I can manage it!"

"Because if not—"

"I can." Ellie cut across her, her cheeks burning as she realized her mistake and saw Matron's eyes narrow. "I'm sorry to interrupt. I just mean, I can do it. I changed dressings all the time at the surgery in Endstone. Thank you so much, Matron. I won't let you down, I promise."

"Hmm, yes, well, we have already discussed how you were overindulged in Endstone. Need I remind you that you are still answerable to Sister Adam here, who is your senior? You will do as she says, swiftly and without complaint."

Ellie dropped her gaze once more as she replied, "Yes, Matron, of course."

"Very well. You will of course be going home this weekend. I trust you will not relearn any of that troublesome pride from spending time with your Endstone admirers, and that you will arrive promptly for your shift on Monday morning. Now, off you go. I have work to do, and so do you."

Ellie felt a bubble of excitement swell in her chest at Matron's words, but she pushed her smile back down until she had nodded, thanked her once more and hurried from the room. Outside, with the door closed firmly behind her, she let the grin stretch towards her ears, as she ran back towards the stairs.

The grin was gone from her face later that morning as she prepared to change the dressings on Private Garrett's many wounds. The injuries she had been used to treating in Endstone – even those of returned soldiers – were far further along in the healing process. She had seen dressings being changed at the hospital many times; witnessed brave grown men breaking down from the pain.

Perhaps reading her thoughts, Private Garrett gave a nervous smile and said, "There's a reason we call it the Agony Wagon, you know." He jerked his head in the direction of the trolley of dressings.

Seeing his anxious expression, Ellie drew herself upright. After everything this man had been through, she couldn't let her own nerves worry him more. She had to make him feel better; that was her job.

"Well, I'm going to see if I can change every one of your dressings without hurting you at all. Do you think I can do it?"

He laughed hoarsely. "I don't know, Nurse. That seems a bit of a tall order."

"It's lucky that I like a challenge, then, isn't it?" Ellie said brightly, gently pushing up his pyjama top to begin work on his biggest wound, the huge cut just below his ribs where he had been hit by shrapnel, and which had had to have several stitches.

She used one hand to pull his skin as taut as possible to limit the tugging as she carefully peeled off the dressing with the other. Private Garrett had his teeth clenched tight and he craned his neck away as she worked, as though he were trying to escape his own body.

"Don't forget to breathe, will you?" Ellie teased gently, earning herself another tight chuckle.

She felt Sister Adam pacing behind her, the other woman's eyes drilling into her back, but Ellie ignored her. Disposing of the used bandages, she turned back to face the young man. "You're from Bournemouth, aren't you, Private Garrett?" she asked, hoping to distract him from his discomfort and herself from the sister's critical gaze.

"Swanage, actually, Nurse," he replied with a wan smile.

"Swanage – that's by the sea, isn't it?" she asked, carefully washing the tight red skin around the stitches with a warm, clean cloth. "Private?" she prompted him, drawing his eyes from where they had been fixed on the angry-looking skin of his torso.

"That's right," he said, staring unblinkingly at her.

She took the warm linseed poultice she had prepared and began to smooth it over the inflamed skin. "I'm from the seaside too: Endstone, it's in Kent. When you're stronger you'll be able to get out and see the sea here in Brighton. There's nothing quite like the sea, is there?"

"Oh, there isn't, Nurse. I can't wait to see it again, dip my toes in."

"Well, you won't have to wait long. Though let's hope it's not too soon or you'll be back in here, having those toes treated for frostbite! Now try not to disturb that poultice while it does its work. I'll just treat these smaller cuts on your arms and legs and then I'll be back in about half an hour to put a clean dressing on your chest."

Private Garrett looked down in surprise. "Blimey! You *are* good!"

Ellie grinned broadly, pretending not to hear the loud tut from behind her.

She worked quickly to change the dressing on the rest of Private Garrett's injuries, then moved on to Corporal Snow. He never complained about anything, but still Ellie moved as gently as she could as she unwound the bandage around his head, and then the dressing over his upper brow.

She deliberately kept her breathing even as she uncovered the wound. Again, this injury was a result of shrapnel; in Corporal Snow's case, it had cracked his skull, causing one of his eyes to droop slightly. The skin was sore and puckered around the stitches. Ellie knew he must be desperately uncomfortable.

As she began to clean the wound, she asked Corporal Snow how he was feeling.

"Oh, fine, my dear, thank you," he said in cheerful tones, though when she glanced down, she saw that his hands were gripping the bedsheets tight where they lay in his lap. "And how are you?"

Ellie smiled to herself. He was always such a gentleman! "I'm very well, thank you. I'm so excited to be able to do a little more to help around here." She laid some clean gauze against the wound.

"Well, my girl, you're a natural." The corporal chuckled. "You look like you're only just out of school, but you act as though you've been treating patients for years!"

Ellie found herself beaming, glad that she was still facing away from Sister Adam. She continued winding the clean bandage around his head. "Thank you, sir, that's so kind of you to say so. I've been lucky enough to have had some excellent teachers. When I was at home I helped out in—"

"*Nurse* Phillips." Sister Adam cut across her sharply. "Would you like me to change the rest of the men's dressings for you? Only you seem to be taking a rather long time and there is a lot more to be done." She gave a hollow laugh.

47

Ellie secured the corporal's bandage with a safety pin, allowed herself a brief roll of the eyes, then keeping her tone resolutely light, she replied, "No, thank you, Sister, that won't be necessary."

She made sure the corporal was comfortable, then hurried on to the next bed. As she worked, she wished fervently that Sister Adam would find something to do outside of the ward. This was certainly the most painstaking and important of all her tasks; she knew how much easier it was to avoid causing the men unnecessary pain if she moved slowly and carefully. But she sensed that the sister was unhappy with this addition to her role, was looking for an excuse to find fault with Ellie, to take this work away from her again.

She briskly changed the dressing on Private Chase's stump, where his left foot had been amputated, and hurried back to remove Private Garrett's poultice and re-dress the wound; then it was Private Das's turn.

Ellie approached nervously. She had given up on trying to make conversation with the soldier, beyond the essentials and the requirements of basic courtesy. Now she mumbled a greeting and let him know that she would start by cleaning the skin around the edge of his leg cast. Unsurprisingly, he made no reply; merely grunted to indicate that he had heard her.

Cleaning around the cast didn't take long; so much of his leg was covered by it that there was little she could do. She moved on to his arm, being careful to keep her gaze away from his face as she worked. Slowly, slowly, she unwrapped the bandage.

"Hurry up, can't you?" Private Das snapped, suddenly.

Ellie froze. It was the first time she had heard his voice properly. It was low; his accent crisp and precise. She looked up at him; his eyes were focused on her, glaring. She wondered if he even recognized who she was.

"I said get on with it, not stop completely!"

"I'm sorry!" Ellie gasped, fumbling with the bandage as she tried to pull the rest of it off. She yanked at the gauze in her hurry and it must have tugged on his damaged skin; he sucked in a sharp breath.

"I'm sorry, I'm sorry," she whispered again. As she glanced up at his face, she was horrified to see that there were tears trickling down from his closed eyes.

Her own hands were shaking violently now; she let go of the gauze and drew in a ragged breath.

He opened his eyes and glowered at her. "Well, what are you waiting for?"

"I . . . I don't want to hurt you."

"It's a little late for that, don't you think?" he hissed in reply.

"What's the problem? Nurse Phillips?" Sister Adam's voice came from close behind her.

"I . . . I . . ."

"Oh, for goodness' sake," the sister barked. "Step aside and I'll finish this off. We can't have patients waiting around in discomfort for you to pull yourself together."

"Yes, Sister," Ellie murmured miserably, her eyes fixed on the floor.

"We need more boiled water. Go and fetch some and then continue with the patients on the other side of the room."

"Yes, Sister," Ellie said again, delighted to have an excuse to leave the ward. She seized the large enamel bowl and hurried from the room, only just containing her hot tears until she was out of sight.

She swung off the corridor and into the nurses' washroom, resting the bowl on the counter, and her hands on the edge of the sink. She stared at her reflection; her eyes and the skin around them red; her jaw set. She turned on the tap and splashed her face with the icy water, again and again. How could she have ever thought she could be a nurse? Maybe sweeping the floor and handing out lunches was all she was fit for. Or maybe she should have just stayed in Endstone all along.

Endstone, she thought. *Jack*. If she could just hang on until the end of the week, she would be back there with him.

Just three more days.

FIVE

MID DECEMBER

As the train rattled into Endstone station, Ellie was already on her feet, having swung her new leather bag, a gift from Aunt Frances, down from the overhead rack. She remembered how she had always looked at Aunt Frances's own weekend bag with envy when she came to visit; had longed for a reason to pack a bag of her own and explore the world beyond Endstone for herself.

Now, after only two months away, she stared out eagerly over the familiar countryside as they approached, remembering as the train drew level with the station how she had passed through this building twice a day when she had been working at the factory. Best of all, though, was the sight of the two figures on the platform: one tall, broad boy, auburn hair curling out from underneath his cap, his left hand clinging to the chubby fist of a small but solid blond boy – in his hand a wooden sign with WELCOME HOME, ELLIE painted in blue. Little clouds emerged from both their mouths with every breath.

Ellie threw open the door before the train had come to a halt and leapt out, dropping her bag on the platform. The icy air seemed to rip the breath from her lungs. She ran for the two boys, stopping just in front of them as she remembered Jack's injured leg, and at the same time feeling overcome by a sudden shyness.

"Lellie!" Charlie cannoned into her legs and she scooped him up, her arms straining at the weight.

"Charlie! Have you got even bigger since I was at home?" she asked, then smothered his cold face with kisses.

"Oof, gettoff, Lellie!" Charlie protested, squirming out of her arms.

"Yeah, Ellie, put me down and all. It's embarrassing for big lads like us," Jack remarked, his mouth quirking upwards on one side. He opened his arms and she stepped into them, resting her cheek against his shoulder, her head underneath his chin.

"You're looking so much better," she said. "Are you off the crutch and everything?"

"Ah, no, not quite," he said, stepping slightly away, while keeping one arm around her, so that he could gesture at his crutch, which was leaning against the wall of the station. "But it was rather ruining the display." She laughed. "I am a lot better, though. Almost back to full strength, which is just as well, since this brother of yours doesn't have much patience with slowcoaches."

As they walked over to retrieve his crutch, Jack looked at Ellie critically. "You're not looking great yourself, though, El." She scowled, pushing back a wisp of hair that had escaped from its pins, and it was his turn to laugh. "Now, don't get cross with me already. I just mean you look tired. Those witches working you too hard?"

"Not really," she replied. "No harder than anyone else. It's fine. They've only just started letting me do any actual nursing. Not that I'll tell Mother that,"

54

she added hastily. "She kept trying to tell me that it wouldn't be glamorous and exciting before I left. I don't want her thinking she was right all along."

"My lips are sealed," Jack said. "I know how insufferable a Phillips woman can be when she thinks she's been proved right— Ouch!" He broke off as she punched him hard in the arm. "Anyway, speaking of your mother, she's expecting us for lunch, so we should get going."

"*Us?*" Ellie asked in surprise.

"That's right, I'm invited too."

"Really?"

"You needn't sound so shocked. You well know how charming I am when you get to know me."

"Yes, I mean, no. . . Oh, be quiet!" she replied in a fluster as he chuckled merrily. But in truth she *was* shocked. Her mother had never made any secret of the fact that she disapproved of Jack and didn't think him suitable company for Ellie. Still, if that had changed, it was a good thing, of course. Ellie shook her head. "Come on, you're right. It will be more than our lives are worth if we're late."

Jack went to pick up her bag, but she stopped him

with a hand on his shoulder. "Don't be silly, Jack, I'll carry that. You need a hand free for your crutch."

It was his turn to scowl. "Oh, I suppose you think I'm less of a man since I had my accident, is that it? I can't carry a bag now?"

"Firstly, I don't think your ability to carry a bag has anything to do with whether you're a man or not. I carried that bag from my digs to the station in Brighton with no trouble, and I'm not a man, I think we can both agree. Secondly. . ." She picked the bag up and began to move towards the station exit. "Secondly, I've never thought you're a man. You're a *boy*." She started to run.

Jack gave a shout of laughter and seized Charlie's hand. "Is that right? Come on, Charlie. Our manhood is in question. I think your sister needs reminding of the pecking order around here."

The boys chased her for a few paces, but then a combination of Jack's bad leg, Charlie's short ones and the encumbrances of Ellie's bag, the welcome home sign and the icy ground caused them to stop by unspoken agreement, laughing breathlessly.

Ellie slid the sign into her bag, slung it over her

left shoulder and took hold of Charlie's hand with her right hand. Jack took hold of his other hand and leaned on his crutch with his right. This odd parade set off along the frost-covered country lane that led from the station, behind the village square and up the hill to the Phillips's house. Charlie kept swinging himself from their hands, making progress even more laborious.

"He normally makes me try to do this all by myself," Jack puffed.

Ellie kept sneaking sidelong glances at him. It was a good job her hands were full or she might have not been able to resist the temptation to reach out and tuck one of his curls behind his ear. He caught her looking and grinned broadly.

"You've been seeing a lot of him, then?" she asked quickly, before he could tease her.

"Oh, yes, myself and Charlie were spending a lot of time together before I started back at work." Jack had recently taken a job at another munitions factory, a little further away from Endstone. "I've been trying to stop in on him and your mam before or after work, when I can too."

"Jack! That's so kind of you!"

"It's nothing. It's only what you'd do if it was my mam and I was away."

This was true, but the situation was not the same at all. Jack's mother Mabel was warm and welcoming; Ellie's mother could not be described that way.

At last they approached the front of the Phillips's house. The garden was bare and the frost sparkled in the pale afternoon light. Ellie could hear the waves crashing beyond the clifftops. At the sight of the familiar building, Ellie felt her tongue go thick in her throat. To her surprise, a warm tear escaped from one eye and trickled down her face.

"El?" Jack said, his voice unusually soft.

"I'm fine, I'm fine." She sniffed loudly and wiped her eyes roughly with her coat sleeve. "I don't know what's wrong with me."

"I have a few suggestions. . ."

She laughed and then had to blow her nose on Jack's proffered handkerchief. "It's just strange coming home . . . and Father not being here. That's silly, I know. It's so long since he's been here. . ."

"Come *on*, Lellie," Charlie interrupted crossly. "S'lunchtime!"

"So it is, Charlie boy," Jack replied, giving Ellie a wink. "Let's go." He pulled her in tight for a quick hug, then the three of them walked up the path.

As they reached the front door, it swung open, revealing Ellie's mother. She was thin and pale, but not, Ellie thought, any more so than usual.

"Hello, Eleanor," she said with her habitual stiffness, but Ellie noticed there was an unfamiliar softness around her mouth.

"Hello, Mother," she said, stepping forward and giving her a kiss on her cheek. She was a little taller than her mother now and had to stoop slightly.

"Come along in. Lunch is ready."

They stepped inside and Ellie dropped her bag at the bottom of the stairs, before she, Jack and Charlie went to wash their hands.

Mother had set the table in the kitchen, including a sprig of winter blooms in a vase in the centre. She had prepared a steak and kidney pie. When Ellie was home her mother usually left the cooking to her, but she was an excellent cook herself and the pie smelled delicious.

Ellie chewed on the inside of her cheek, feeling another wave of tears threaten.

"Sit down, sit down."

They all sat and settled down to their meal.

"How are you, Mother?" Ellie asked, as she spooned some green beans on to Charlie's plate, ignoring his glower.

"I'm somewhat better today, thank you," Mother said a little reluctantly. "I woke early so I thought I would make a pie while I was feeling stronger. But my migraines have been very bad lately. It has been such a strain having to care of Charlie all by myself when I'm so unwell."

Ellie squirmed guiltily.

"Shall I get some milk from the pantry, Mrs Phillips?" Jack asked, giving Ellie a gentle kick under the table.

"Oh, yes, please, Jack," said Mother, offering him a tight smile. Ellie felt her mouth drop open and quickly snapped it shut again.

"Some of the other ladies from the WI are helping out, though, aren't they?" he called, from the pantry. "And Sarah Pritchard?" Sarah was the oldest child of Dr Mertens. She had married the young doctor Thomas Pritchard in the summer of that year. A kind, warm girl, she loved children, and had offered to help Mother out with Charlie whenever she wasn't needed in the surgery.

"Well . . . yes," Mother replied. "But still . . ."

"Sounds like Ellie's been working very hard at the hospital too," Jack continued cheerfully, returning and pouring them each a glass of milk. "I suppose we're all having to take on new responsibilities the longer the war goes on."

Ellie glanced at him nervously. She hoped he wouldn't mention the money – the vast majority of her tiny expenses allowance that she was sending home each week. Mother thought it unspeakably vulgar to talk about money, and hated any acknowledgement of the difficult situation the family was in financially.

"The pie is delicious, Mother," she said quickly, before the conversation could turn in any undesirable direction.

"Well, as you know, meat is scarce, but I thought you might need sustenance. Goodness knows, Frances has never been any great cook."

"Oh, the landlady cooks for us most days," Ellie said, seizing on this new topic. "She's really very good. Not that she's made anything this tasty," she added hastily. "It is a lovely treat to have some home cooking."

"Very good, Mrs Phillips," Jack agreed, with a sigh of satisfaction. "Thank you."

"You're welcome, Jack. There is plenty left. You should have some more."

Again, Ellie found herself staring. For her whole life, as long as she had been friends with Jack, she had had to beg Mother for him to be allowed even to cross the threshold. And yet here was Mother welcoming him to the table, encouraging him to eat more, looking at him with an expression both disapproving but also . . . almost fond, as though he wasn't eating enough (never truly a risk with Jack, when food was available), and as though this were somehow her responsibility.

Jack caught her gaze and gave her a wink when Mother wasn't looking. "Thank you, Mrs Phillips, I think I might. Can I get anyone else more while I'm up?"

Ellie and her mother both shook their heads but Charlie shouted, "More, please, Jack!"

"Wait a minute, Charlie," Ellie said, tousling his

curls. "You haven't eaten your beans yet, and you've just mushed your pastry up."

"Oh, let him have more, El," Jack said, putting another small slice on to Charlie's plate without waiting for a response. "He's a growing lad, aren't you, Charlie boy?"

Charlie just grinned, revealing a stuffed mouth. Ellie glanced at Mother to see if she would raise an objection, but she was smiling indulgently. Ellie felt her own brow becoming more furrowed by the second. What was going on here?

Jack and Ellie cleared up the lunch things together, while Mother went for a lie-down.

"Come on, El, let's go for a walk around the village," Jack said, hanging the tea towel to dry over the range.

"Charlie—"

"Is playing happily. He's not a baby any more, you know. He's fine entertaining himself while your mam's in the house. Come on." He took her by the hand and tugged her into the hallway, thrusting her coat into her arms.

"Ever the gentleman."

"You know me!" He gave her a wide grin.

Having checked in on Charlie, while Jack rolled his eyes, they set off out of the house. Already the sun had passed its highest point in the sky and was beginning its descent, giving the light a creamy quality.

Jack took her gloved hand in his own, threading their fingers together. Ellie felt an answering puddle of warmth in her stomach, but her mind was still engaged with less pleasant matters.

"I thought Mother was really unwell! I thought I was needed here!"

"She is," Jack replied, swinging her arm. "You are."

"She's not any worse than usual."

"No, but usual isn't great for her, is it? And you know it comes and goes. I don't think you need to worry; she has lots of people keeping an eye on her."

"But yet everyone thought it was so important for me to come back!"

"Knowing you were coming was what got her out of bed and baking that pie, El. That's no mean feat. Anyway, I didn't think it was such a hardship for you to come back to us every so often," he teased gently.

"It's not!" she exclaimed, then consciously softened her tone. "It's really not." She gave his hand a squeeze. "It's just . . . Matron is such a stickler for . . . well, everything. I don't like to ask her for a favour so early."

"A favour? Surely even top nurses get a day off every so often?"

"Well. . ."

"Did she mind? Did she make it difficult for you?"

"Well, no. . ."

"There!"

They fell silent as they approached the village square. Seeing some people in the distance, and under the pretence of scratching her nose, Ellie tugged her hand away, then replaced it in her pocket. She glanced sidelong at Jack to see if he minded, but if anything his grin was wider than ever.

"Anyway," she said jostling him with her elbow, "I'm not a top nurse. I told you; if I'm top anything, it's a top sweeper and lunch distributor."

"Hey, if I was in that hospital, the person giving me my lunch would be the most important person to me!"

Ellie giggled. "Well, that's you. . ."

"You ask those lads. I bet most of them would say

the same thing. And I thought you'd been promoted now; top dressing-changer too, aren't you?"

Ellie waved at Mrs Anderson, who was walking in the church graveyard, but her expression darkened. "I'm definitely not top at that. I told you about what happened with that Indian boy ... well, man ... didn't I?"

"Oh, *he's* a man, is he?" Seeing her scowl, Jack relented. "You can't let one bloke knock your confidence like that, El." They reached the path that led to the woods; one of their favourite places to go together. Jack jerked his head questioningly and Ellie nodded. "You know you're good at taking care of people. Your dad always said so. Thomas says so. So does Dr Mertens." He clambered up the stile and paused with one leg over it. "I think we even came close to you admitting it yourself once." He hopped down and held his hand out to her from the other side. "Whatever's going on with this chap, it's his business not yours."

Ellie looked pointedly at his outstretched hand and then raised one eyebrow. Taking a couple of steps back, she ran, braced her hands against the wooden planks

66

and vaulted over, landing with a squelch and a splatter of mud beside him. She smiled up at him sweetly.

Jack was sucking his cheeks and chewing his tongue to try to stifle his own smile. He gave up with a bark of laughter which sent something flapping in alarm through the branches nearby.

"Well, I'm glad to see you haven't become a city girl entirely," he said, when he could next catch his breath.

By way of an answer she merely wiggled her eyebrows – which set him off in another helpless wave of giggles – and marched ahead through the slushy leaves. When he caught up with her again, still breathing unevenly from the laughter, she thrust her hand back into his before she could think herself out of it. She felt him glance at her, but stared fixedly ahead as she said, "Have you heard much from Will lately?"

Will was Jack's older brother who had been away at war for a couple of years; he'd joined up at the same time as Ellie's father. Jack had run away to join him last year, but had soon been discovered and sent home on account of being too young.

"Not for a couple of weeks, but then we had a few

letters close together, when they were stationed away from the front line."

"Is he well?"

"Sounds it. I still can't believe how he's adjusted to being out there . . . the things he has to do . . . the things he sees. It's like he's a different person from the one who left home."

"I feel as though we're all different people from a few years ago." Ellie knew that Jack had been shocked by how hard he'd found the front line himself. All his life, he'd been the more robust of the brothers; the braver, tougher, louder and more confident one; the one who couldn't wait to join up when the war started. But in reality, when he was actually there, in France, facing real guns, real poison gas and real bombs, seeing fear and death all around him, he'd found the army a living nightmare; had revealed only to Ellie his secret relief at being sent home when his true age had been discovered.

His thoughts were obviously running along the same track as hers, as he now said, "I'm not looking forward to going back out there myself, but I know I must, before too long."

"No, Jack," Ellie protested, turning slightly to look at him. They had arrived in their favourite clearing, by the tree where Ellie had buried some of her father's things after he died. "You've still got almost two years before you're old enough to be called up."

"I know, El, I know that's true technically. But we both also know I'm stronger and fitter than lots of the lads who are out there already. Or, at least, I will be once my leg is back to strength," he went on hurriedly, seeing she was about to argue. "I don't want to fight with you about this again, Ellie. You're doing your bit, helping out with the lads that come back – and you're technically too young for that, aren't you? Well, I'm no good at doctoring. Physical work is what I can do, is all I've ever been able to do." They had stopped and were facing each other now. He put his gloved hand to her mouth to silence the latest contradiction she was about to voice. "What you're doing is so important, but if the soldiers could just win this blasted war then you wouldn't need to be patching men back together; people wouldn't need to lose their dads or their brothers or their husbands."

Ellie wasn't sure she agreed that it was down to

the soldiers. But it was hard to argue with what Jack was saying. She looked up into his unusually serious face.

"Please, El. It's hard enough to convince myself. Arguing with you is like having a fight with my own shadow; please don't make me do it." He removed his hand from her mouth, but slowly, and with a stern expression.

"All right," she whispered. "But just . . . not yet. *Please*. Wait until your leg is back to normal, at least. For my sake, Jack. I know I've not been there, but I've seen more of the men that come back than you have. It was bad enough when you were away before. Now that I work in the hospital, I think I'd spend the whole time imagining things that might happen to you."

"El. . ."

"*Please*, Jack. I'm not asking you not to go at all. Just wait a bit. Who knows, maybe the end of the war really is around the corner now. Surely it can't go on for ever!"

They looked at each other, neither voicing the thought that maybe it could, maybe neither side would ever give up and this was how the world would end;

with the fighting just going on and on until there was no one left on either side.

"All right, El," Jack said at last, his voice sounding husky. "I'll wait a bit longer."

He wrapped his arms around her, his hands clasped at the base of her spine, and drew her in closer to him. Leaning down, he rested his forehead against hers. This close, his periwinkle eyes swam before her, his freckles all seeming to blur together. She twined her arms around his neck and closed her eyes, feeling a glimmer of winter sun through her eyelids, making everything a deep red. She felt a light brush against her lips and her eyes flickered open for a moment before she kissed him back.

They had kissed once, just once before, in the immediate aftermath of the explosion at the factory. For some time, Ellie had felt the sands of their friendship shifting, the kiss seeming to be the ultimate expression of that. But they had never spoken about it since and the kiss hadn't been repeated. Until now. Suddenly desperate for it not to end, Ellie reached up on to the balls of her feet, tightening her grip around his neck. She felt his lips curling into a smile, felt a rumble of laughter in his chest, but she didn't release him for several moments more.

When she did, they were both struggling a little to catch their breath, and his cheeks had the vivid stripes of red they always displayed when he was angry or flustered or hot. She smiled and put her hand to one cheek. He grinned back at her, then tugged her closer and dropped a kiss on the top of her head.

"Come on, Nurse Phillips, let's get you home."

The next two days went far too quickly. Ellie called in to the surgery and to Jack's mother's shop. She visited old, crotchety Miss Webb, and went again to the spot she had chosen in lieu of a grave for her father, where she sat and told him all about her experiences as a real nurse. And of course she spent as much time as she could with her mother and Charlie, and Jack. It was hard for her and Jack to get any time alone together, but he seemed happy just to accompany her on her errands and visits whenever his work allowed. And she was happy to have him with her.

Sunday evening came around too quickly. After a last meal, Ellie said goodbye to her mother and, with tears on both sides, to Charlie. Then she and Jack set off on their bicycles to the station. A light rain was falling as they cycled but they scarcely noticed, content to ride slowly alongside one another, continuing the almost constant flow of conversation they had kept up for the whole weekend.

Ellie was talking about Private Das once more. "I won't let him knock my confidence again. It's like you said, I wouldn't be there at all if I weren't fit to be a nurse. And it's what I *want* to do. But still, I can't help but wonder about him. I'm sure he wouldn't be this unfriendly if there weren't something bothering him. I mean, besides the fact that he's in so much pain. I just feel that if I knew what it was, I might be able to help. I expect homesickness has something to do with it. I've been feeling it enough myself and I'm still in the same country, not even that far from home. I can't even imagine what it must feel like for him. I'd love to talk to him about his home too. What it's like there. It must be so different—"

"Yes, well." Jack broke across her. "You'll soon be back there and able to ask him all about it, won't you?"

Ellie glanced at him curiously. It was unlike him to be so snappish. "Except that I'm sure he still won't want to speak to me," she said with a little laugh. She found herself strangely relieved to see the station building ahead of them.

They arrived and leaned their bicycles against the wall. Jack was going to come back and collect Ellie's the next day.

They could hear the rumble of the train in the distance. Ellie took Jack's hands in hers. "I'll miss you. I always do, you know."

"I miss you too," he replied, still a little gruffly.

The train squealed in behind them and Ellie reached up to kiss him, feeling her cheeks flush at the thought of the people already on the train watching. She hefted her bag, waving away his offer of help, and climbed on to the train. She remaining standing, her hand raised to wave as the train lurched back into motion and began to move out of the station. She stood peering out of the window until even the station building itself was only a speck on the horizon.

SIX

APPROACHING CHRISTMAS

Despite a fluttering echo of her first-day nerves in her stomach, Ellie found she was pleased to return to the hospital the next morning; to put on her uniform, have breakfast in Mrs Joyce's kitchen with Aunt Frances while filling her in on the news from Endstone, and then march briskly through the damp Brighton streets on her now-familiar route to work. As she walked she glanced around her at the bustling figures heading for their places of employment and smiled with pleasure to be one of them.

Arriving at the hospital, she stowed her coat and bag in the cloakroom, then bid Aunt Frances goodbye and hurried up to her ward, keen to see how the patients were doing and to catch up on any developments that might have occurred while she was away. For the first time, it crossed her mind that one of the men might have been discharged, or moved to a different ward or even hospital. She didn't let herself think for more than a moment about the fact that any of their conditions might have worsened. How awful it would be not to have said goodbye one of the men, most of whom had begun to feel like old friends.

She needn't have worried; as she walked into the room, tightening the strings of her apron, twelve familiar faces looked up her as one. Even better, there was no sign of Sister Adam.

"Nurse Phillips, you're back!" called Private Garrett with a whoop, and there were similar cries of delighted greeting from the other men.

Ellie smiled broadly, moving to fetch her broom. As she did so, she couldn't help her gaze from flickering in the direction of Private Das's corner, and she was startled to discover that her instinct had been right; he too had looked up to see her when she came in. For a fraction of a second, their eyes locked and Ellie felt her stomach clench like a squeezed fist, before he looked away again.

As she began sweeping, she asked the men if there was any news.

"What have I missed?" she demanded cheerfully, having glanced round to confirm that Sister Adam still hadn't appeared. "Wheelchair races in the corridor? Something other than potato soup for lunch?" She took one more careful look around. "Somebody managing to make Sister Adam smile?"

The men burst out in shouts of laughter.

"Chance would be a fine thing," Private Garrett guffawed wheezily. "That one is sour all the way through. Like an under-ripe apple. Not a drop of the festive spirit in her."

"Well, really," Ellie said, with a grin, "I'd have thought charming fellows such as yourselves would have no excuse for not succeeding. You're clearly not trying hard enough. Perhaps you should serenade her with Christmas carols."

As she passed Corporal Snow's bed, she noticed he was struggling to sit up. She helped him to prop his pillows so that he could.

"Ah, my dear, we have missed you and your cheerfulness. The place has just not been the same. Of course, Nurse Boyle is a true tonic, but when she's not on duty, well. . ."

She patted the corporal on the shoulder. He was too much of a gentleman to say anything negative about Sister Adam, but his meaning was clear. "I've missed you all too," she replied.

He chuckled. "It's kind of you to say so, my dear, but I'm sure a bright young thing like you has been far too busy at home to miss our ragtag bunch. How are your family?"

"They're well, thank you for asking, Corporal," Ellie said, raising her voice so she could still be heard as she crouched under the next bed, Corporal Putt's, to catch the eddies of dust that had gathered beneath it. "My mother seemed in much better health by the time I left."

"I'm sure seeing you helped a great deal," the softly spoken corporal murmured. Ellie thought of her mother's cool demeanour and smiled wryly. Then she remembered Jack saying Mother had got out of bed especially to make her the pie. She said, "Maybe,

Corporal. She has plenty of good people taking care of her there, anyway."

"And how's that little brother of yours?" Sergeant Barry asked as she approached. He had two small boys of his own, and Ellie had noticed that he always liked to hear about Charlie, as though that would bring his sons nearer. She thought of how the men had already been away from home for so long, and how they would almost certainly have to spend Christmas in the hospital. Ellie passed the sergeant a glass of water as his painful cough started up once more.

"Oh, Sergeant, he's getting so big!" she replied. "Honestly, he's grown so much in the couple of months I've been away." Seeing the sergeant's sad expression, she hurried on. "But really, it's no wonder, with the amount he eats. I've seen him almost keep pace with boys thirteen years older than him! And these are boys known for the size of their own appetites, mind!" She smiled, thinking of Jack and Charlie at the table together, and the sergeant gave a croaky laugh into his handkerchief.

"He has a tricycle but he clearly thinks he's far too grown up for it now. He insisted we let him try my bicycle," she continued, wanting to keep the sergeant smiling. "Of course, his legs are nowhere near long enough so I had to run by his side the whole time to be ready to catch him. And then he was outraged when I did – I'd offended his pride, don't you know!"

A sharp voice cut across the men's laughter: "Nurse Phillips, perhaps you've forgotten while you were away having a holiday – this is a hospital. It's a place of rest and recuperation. Kindly keep your rowdy stories for your leisure time."

Ellie caught Sergeant Barry's eye and gave him a quick wink before turning to face a scowling Sister Adam. "Of course, Sister. I'm sorry."

"I wish I didn't have to say the same things to you over and over. Honestly, I'm growing tired of the sound of my own voice."

Ellie affected an innocent and distressed expression, and adopted a tone to match. "Oh, I am sorry to hear that. I personally associate the sound of your voice with another much appreciated opportunity for me to learn from you and better my practice as a nurse."

Sister Adam narrowed her eyes so far that she must have scarcely been able to see anything through them.

Ellie was careful to keep her face honest and open. She watched the sister struggle and at last give up; it was impossible to find fault when Ellie was more or less echoing back her own words. The sister might have known that she wasn't being entirely straightforward, but with no hint on the girl's face or in her voice there was nothing she could do.

"No one likes a toady, Phillips," she snapped at last. "Stop wasting time and get on with your work."

"Yes, Sister." Ellie smiled sweetly. She knew she was exploiting the fact that she was so much more popular with the men than Sister Adam was; she was edging dangerously close to bullying the older nurse, but it was just so hard to swallow Sister Adam's constant criticism without responding in any way. And she felt so positive on returning to the hospital, she was determined not to let the ward sister make her doubt herself again.

She sighed contentedly as she finished sweeping the room and checking the alignment of the beds, carefully avoiding Private Das's eye as she did so, not wanting to spoil her good mood. As she moved to fetch the trolley of dressings, she glanced nervously at Sister Adam but the older woman was engrossed in measuring out pills into different paper cups for each of the men. Ellie began the process of changing the men's dressings, moving quickly and confidently in the hope that if she was half finished by the time the sister noticed, she would leave her to it. Visiting the surgery in Endstone had been a good idea; whatever Matron's thoughts on what she called Ellie's "Endstone admirers", Ellie had needed the reminder that she was good at this; that while the injuries might be more severe than she was used to dealing with, she knew exactly how to handle them.

She did, however, feel her calm waver a little as she approached Private Das's bed again. Straightaway she could sense that something had changed, though. It was hard to identify what exactly; he still didn't speak to her or meet her eye, but he wasn't making such a point of looking away, and he even shifted a little on his bed so that she could reach his arm more easily.

She didn't speak to him either, merely started to unwrap his bandages slowly, determined to complete the task without incident this time. The ward was peaceful now, the only sounds the gentle murmur of the other men's conversation and the rattle of Sister Adam distributing the pills. Wintry sunlight poured in through the big windows, pooling on the floor and throwing soft shadows of the men in their beds. Ellie relaxed into her work.

"I have a little brother too." Private Das's voice came as such a surprise that Ellie felt herself startle. She raised her eyes to his; he was looking levelly at her, though the twisting of the sheets between his hands revealed his anxiety. Ellie felt a sudden urge to rest her own calming hand on them, but instead she dragged her attention back to his injured arm. "I think perhaps he is the same age as your Charlie," he went on. "Three and a half?" His voice was soft but steady.

Ellie struggled to speak for a moment. Then she cleared her throat. "Yes, that is exactly the same age as Charlie. What's your brother's name?"

"Arun." He paused, then smiled; just the slightest smile but it changed his face completely, opening it up in a way that Ellie had never seen before. "It means 'sun', which is appropriate because my mother thinks he is the source of all light and warmth in the world."

Ellie felt herself smiling too as she carefully cleaned his wound. "That sounds exactly like my Charlie. He can do no wrong as far as my par—" She stumbled over her words but quickly corrected herself. "As far as my mother is concerned. Where is your brother now?"

Private Das dropped his eyes and Ellie found herself staring at those thick eyelashes. "He is at home in Delhi. My whole family is there. It feels like a long way away." His voice had become so quiet again that Ellie had to lean forwards to hear him properly.

Without thinking what she was doing, she put down the damp cloth and rested her hand on top of his. Her breathing sped up as she waited for him to push her away, but for what felt like the longest time, he didn't move at all. Then slowly, so slowly, he lifted his eyes again. They shimmered, but the tears didn't spill. One corner of his mouth turned up in what was almost a smile.

Ellie let out a breath and picked up the cloth again. "Tell me more about Arun," she said, her voice coming out just above a whisper.

So he did. He told her that he was from a family of all boys; there were three more brothers between himself and Arun. Arun was the adored baby of the family; cosseted and coddled by all his doting brothers, as well as by his mother and grandmother, who lived with them. Private Das – "Sanjay," he muttered shyly – had always liked to take Arun to play in Coronation Park when he was home. They would play cricket with all his other brothers, though Arun was too little to be able to bat properly.

The more Ellie heard, the more she wanted to know. She squeezed her eyes closed for a moment, trying to picture this city so far away, where it was hotter than she could imagine for so much of the year, where monsoon rains flooded the streets at other times and the women wore silk saris of every colour conceivable. Delhi sounded like a much, much bigger city than Brighton – which was the largest city Ellie herself had any experience of – and yet it was strange how many aspects of life there sounded just the same. Family, school, work, friends, and the impact of the war; these were the things Private Das's life at home revolved around, just the same as Ellie's own.

"Tick tock, tick tock, Nurse Phillips. Yet again I have to wonder if you need someone else to complete your tasks for you?" Sister Adam's voice called Ellie back into the room abruptly. "There is still much to be done while you're taking for ever over the most basic tasks."

Ellie frowned. She felt as though she'd been lying in the sun in her favourite clearing in the Endstone woods, and a cloud had passed across the sky, rendering everything suddenly cold and dark.

Still, she was careful to make her expression friendly as she turned to the sister. "Almost finished here, Sister Adam. Then I'll get on and sort out Private Brown's dressings."

"See that you do," came the sister's curt reply as she rapped her pencil against her clipboard.

Ellie turned back and smiled apologetically at Private Das – Sanjay, she reminded herself, longing to ask him what his name meant but not daring to under the sister's surveillance. She fixed the new bandage on his leg securely in place, before tidying everything she had finished with up on to the trolley.

"Why does that woman speak like a clock?" he whispered to her as she drew close to the top of the bed. "Do you think perhaps she needs some medical attention herself? I was studying to be a doctor before I left India; I have a few courses of treatment I could recommend."

Ellie suddenly found she had to pay urgent attention to the supplies on the lower shelf of the trolley, as a wave of giggles threatened to expose both her and Sanjay to Sister Adam's suspicious glare.

SEVEN

APRIL, 1917

"Come along, then," Ellie said brightly to Sanjay as she approached his bed. "I expected to find you up and raring to go."

It was April and the days were once again becoming brighter and longer. Sanjay's arm was now completely healed and his leg was much better too. All that remained was to build up his strength; after months of being bedbound, the muscle in his leg had wasted away almost entirely and the joints were stiff. It would be some time before he could use it as he had done before his injury.

The doctors had agreed that the best thing for

the private at this stage in his treatment was short walks once a day in the hospital grounds, to get him using the leg again and breathing fresh sea air. Since the first day that they had spoken properly, Ellie and Sanjay's friendship had grown steadily. She was only too happy to have the responsibility of taking him on his walks.

"Well, Nurse Phillips, it is not so easy for me to be raring to go. I thought it was your job to help me get ready."

"So grumpy!" she teased, crouching down to help him on with his shoes. "I'm terribly sorry the service here isn't up to your standards, milord."

"So you should be," he said with a small grin.

She stood and, taking his hands, pulled him gently to his feet. She guided his arms into his dressing gown and he pulled the cord around the middle tight. Finally, she handed him his crutches and they began their slow progress out of the ward. Sister Adam pretended not to see them as they shuffled past, but her sour expression betrayed her.

It took them at least five minutes to get down the stairs and out into the hospital gardens. In addition to

Sanjay's weakened and painful leg, his general fitness was depleted after months of inactivity, and he became quickly out of breath.

At last they reached the gardens. The sea breeze lifted the tendrils of hair that had escaped from Ellie's bun. She closed her eyes to feel the spring sunshine on her eyelids.

"Brrr!" Her eyes snapped back open at Sanjay's voice. "So cold!" He was huddled in his dressing gown as though an icy wind were blowing.

"This is warm for England!" she exclaimed. "Especially in April!"

"I hate the cold," he said with a shudder as they began to walk. "I think out of all the dreadful things in the trenches, the cold was the worst. That and the damp. It was everywhere. It was impossible to stay dry and so it was impossible to get warm."

Ellie shivered in sympathy. "It sounds horrible."

"It was. So horrible I sometimes wonder if it really happened to me. Or if I'm really here now. Sometimes I think I might wake up and find myself slumped against the mud wall of the trench, rats running over my feet, my boots soaked and water running off the edge of my helmet and down my neck. I don't know what I'll do if I have to go back there," he went on. "Now that the Americans have joined the war, I just hope it will all be over quickly. Or at least that my leg won't be fully better before it is." His eyes slid over to her. "I suppose you think that's cowardly of me?"

"Not at all!" Ellie replied indignantly, taking his elbow to steer him along the left prong of a fork in the path. "Why would you think that? The more I see of the war, the less I can understand anyone *wanting* to go. And it will be better for every one of us – Germans included – when it's all over."

He glanced at her curiously. "I don't hear many of your countrymen and women expressing that sort of view," he remarked.

"No, I know. I just can't understand it. War seems to make perfectly normal, sensible people think very strangely indeed." She paused. "Or maybe I'm the strange one."

"You certainly are very strange," he agreed solemnly and she treated him to a mock scowl. They both laughed.

"What's truly strange is us walking together,

talking and laughing," Ellie continued, a little shyly now. "When I first met you, I thought you hated me. You wouldn't even look at me!"

"Don't!" he said, screwing his eyes tight shut for a moment. "Please, don't. I hate to think of it. I was so rude!"

"You seemed . . . very unhappy," Ellie ventured.

"I was. I think . . . I don't know. It's like I said – I couldn't stop thinking about the trenches. It might sound odd but I became even more homesick when I got here to Brighton. I suppose I didn't have time to think about it when I was in the trenches. And at least among my own company I had some friends. But here I was surrounded by strangers – and though the men on our ward have grown used to me now, I know some of them found it uncomfortable to be side by side with . . . a foreigner. And I couldn't even move out of my bed! I felt angry, though I couldn't have told you with whom. I just got a bit stuck . . . in my own head."

"I understand," Ellie said softly.

"Do you? I'm not sure it really excuses my behaviour. Once I'd started being rude to you, it became even more difficult to turn around and start behaving as a gentleman ought. I thought *you* must hate *me* by then."

Ellie smiled at him. He was facing into the sunshine, and it gave his eyes an amber glow as the light glanced off them. "Really, Sanjay, it's fine," she said. They had stopped and she rested her hand over his on top of the crutch, giving it a gentle squeeze. "You don't have to explain. What you've lived through. . ." She trailed off, thinking of Jack and how changed he had been when he had first returned from the front line. But the thought of Jack caused her a pang of guilt, so she pushed it aside and ploughed on. "Anyway," she said, her tone lighter, "I'm glad you decided to start behaving 'as a gentleman ought'. And now we're old friends, aren't we?"

Many months after she had first seen it, his smile still always caught her by surprise. It made her think of that moment when, puffing up to the clifftops at home, the sea would suddenly come into view, sunlight glinting off it in a way that made it look like silver silk or a bright new coin.

"We are."

"Well, then, old friend," she went on, forcing a note of jollity into her voice, "on to serious business. What is the word of the day?"

"The word of the day? Ah. . ."

"Don't tell me you haven't thought of one!"

Sanjay intended to continue his training as a doctor after the war finished and had a huge amount of medical knowledge already from his earlier training, as well as from his constant reading. He and Ellie had begun a game in which he quizzed her on what she knew of various different medical terms and conditions – with a different word each day. She loved learning from him; he was a good teacher, patient and intelligent, with an answer for all of her questions. In many ways he reminded Ellie of her father – except in one thing: she sensed that Sanjay rather enjoyed showing off what he knew, and gently correcting her whenever he had the opportunity.

"Patience, Nurse Phillips, patience," he pretended to scold her. "You wouldn't think of rushing Sister Adam in this way, would you?" He made a great show of looking around nervously. "Or . . . *Matron*."

Ellie giggled. "No, sir. Sorry, sir!"

"That's better. Now, class, the word for the day is *appendicitis*. What can you tell me about the causes, symptoms and treatment?"

They had reached the bench furthest from the hospital, which faced out over the sea. Ellie helped Sanjay to sit, taking his crutches from him as she repeated, "*Appendicitis*. . ." She sat down next to him. "Appendicitis is the painful swelling of the appendix," she began eagerly, "which is a sort of pouch attached to the small intestine whose function within the body is not known for certain." She glanced at Sanjay; his expression was neutral. "Likewise, the causes of appendicitis are not clear, but it would seem it that it is often brought about by . . . er . . . waste material" – she felt herself blushing and hurried on before Sanjay could notice – "or a swollen lymph node within the wall of the bowel blocking the entrance to it. To the appendix, that is. This blockage can lead to inflammation and swelling, which, if the pressure becomes sufficiently great, can lead to the appendix rupturing."

She looked again at Sanjay and he inclined his head, gesturing for her to go on. She sucked in a breath. "Symptoms are pain in the abdomen, becoming concentrated over time on the lower right-hand side, the site of the appendix, and becoming constant and severe."

"And how might a medical practitioner confirm diagnosis?" Sanjay asked her, clasping his hands on top of one of his crutches and resting his chin on them, gazing levelly at her.

"Er. . . The pain becomes worse when the area is pressed upon, or when the patient walks or coughs. Other symptoms can include loss of appetite and nausea."

"And, on occasion, diarrhoea," Sanjay put in in neutral tones.

"Yes, and diarrhoea," Ellie said, cross to feel herself blushing again. For heaven's sake, she couldn't get embarrassed about basic bodily functions if she wished to be a proper nurse!

"And what of the treatment?" Sanjay asked now.

"In most cases, the appendix will need to be removed through surgery."

"Hmm, good," Sanjay said, causing Ellie to beam with pleasure. "Do you know what other treatments have been attempted in the past?"

"Ah. . ." Ellie's mind skittered around. She had had Thomas send many of her father's old medical textbooks to her in Brighton, and had been attempting to read as much as she could each night before she fell asleep, as well as during any time off. Still, it felt like there was always more she didn't know, even for such common illnesses as appendicitis.

"In the past, drainage of the appendix was often attempted, with varying degrees of success," said Sanjay. "But now, as you say, and especially given the apparently non-essential nature of the appendix, it is generally considered to be better to simply remove it before it can cause more problems."

Ellie nodded, feeling oddly downcast that she hadn't been able to answer all of his questions.

"And tell me, Ellie, which patients that you might encounter are more likely than others to be suffering from appendicitis?"

Again, Ellie cast around in the recesses of her brain for something useful. "Er . . . one in thirteen people are likely to suffer from appendicitis at some point in their life. . ."

"Yes," Sanjay said, still with complete patience,

which somehow managed to make Ellie feel more panicked. "But in terms of which patients are more likely to experience it at any given time, it is, of course, possible at any age, but more common in those between the ages of ten and twenty."

"Oh," said Ellie glumly. No matter how long she had spent searching the alcoves and corners of her mind, she would never have come across that fact. How did Sanjay retain so much, in a language that wasn't even his first?

"You did well, Ellie," Sanjay said. "But there is always more to read."

"Yes," she said miserably, "but how can one read it all? And even if you do, how can you remember it?"

"It is tricky," Sanjay conceded, though it was clearly not tricky for him. "And of course you are busy with and tired from your work. Do not be too hard on yourself." The skin around his eyes crinkled.

Ellie shrugged. Sanjay leaned across and tugged on another strand of hair that had burst free, reminding Ellie again of Jack. "The human brain is an incredible thing, Nurse Phillips. Keep nourishing it with hearty food and you will be astounded by the results."

Ellie smiled. She could almost feel her brain stretching with every moment she spent with him.

"Nurse Phillips!" came a voice from behind them.

They turned to see Matron's stout form striding across the garden. "Nurse Phillips," she repeated as she drew closer, "I believe that is enough fresh air for today. We don't want Private Das catching a chill, do we?"

"No, Matron," Ellie said, chastened. "I will bring him back in at once."

"Humph," was all the response that came, but Ellie felt Matron watching them beadily as they progressed slowly across the lawn towards the hospital building.

"Well, you certainly gave her what-for," muttered Sanjay, leaning his head close to Ellie's.

She laughed once more, glancing round to see if Matron was still watching. She was, but this only made Ellie's giggles worse. This time, as they clambered laboriously back up the stairs, it was Ellie who had to keep stopping to catch her breath between gales of uncontrollable laughter. Each time, Sanjay shook his head and tutted at her, but he couldn't contain his own grin.

At last they made it back to the ward. Ellie ran her hand over her face as though it would remove her smile before Sister Adam objected to it.

She settled Sanjay back into his bed, removing his shoes and dressing gown first.

"I look forward to tomorrow's test," Sanjay murmured to her, as she leaned his crutches alongside the bed.

"So do I," she replied, resolving to ransack Aunt Frances's supply of medical books as well as her father's that night.

That evening, Ellie felt so tired she could barely lift her feet to get herself home. The final hill on her approach always threatened to be her undoing and today she found herself slumped against a lamp post, staring at the pavement for several seconds before she could muster the strength to continue.

"Come along!" she told herself firmly. At this rate she would fall asleep in her dinner without reading a word of any of the medical books.

At last she reached the front door. She jiggled the key in the lock and pushed the door open. As she shrugged off her jacket, her eye was immediately drawn to the envelope addressed to her that waited on the dresser.

The wave of guilt she had pushed aside earlier came flooding back. Jack. She had found it harder and harder to find time to write to him in recent weeks. Even when she wasn't working or sleeping, she was frantically trying to catch up with her reading so that she could stand a chance of being ahead of Sanjay in the next day's challenge. Despite finding it onerous, Jack had continued to write at least once a week, updating her on all his news, and that of his family and hers. She knew that she would miss these regular bulletins if she didn't receive them, but as it was they made her feel remorseful for her own lack of communication.

Still standing in the hallway, Ellie pressed her fingertips against her eyebrows. In many ways, it would just be easier if she didn't have to think about home. If she could only concentrate on her work and her life here, she might manage to keep on top of things. She wondered if her father and Jack had felt that like this when they were away at war.

"Oh, hello, dear." Mrs Joyce seemed surprised to find Ellie in the hallway. "I didn't hear you come in. You look worn out! Why don't you go and get out of your work clothes and then I'll have dinner on the table for you? I presume Frances is going to be late again today?"

Ellie roused herself to reply. "Yes, I think so. Thank you, Mrs Joyce, I'll do that."

She thrust the letter, unopened, into the pocket at the front of her apron and ran up the stairs. If she had a quick dinner now, she might have time for an hour's reading before bed.

EIGHT

MAY, 1917

In the nurses' washroom, Ellie clambered out of her uniform, fumbling slightly as she folded each item in turn and made a little pile of the clothes. From her bag, she took out a clean skirt and blouse, and put them on carefully. She put the uniform into her bag and, picking up this and her navy cardigan, she left the cubicle.

She was washing her face when Grace emerged from another cubicle.

The other girl smiled at her as she began to wash her hands in a neighbouring sink. "Are you looking forward to your afternoon off?" she asked.

Her words were friendly but Ellie felt – and saw, in

the mirror – herself blushing furiously. "Yes," she said, her tone more defensive than she would have liked. "Who doesn't look forward to an afternoon off?"

"Oh, I know," Grace agreed readily, showing no sign of offence. "I'm dead envious – I'm only starting my shift now!"

Ellie dried her hands on the towel, taking advantage of the moment to regain her poise. She knew the other girl had only meant kindly, but she was beginning to regret telling anybody about her plans for the afternoon. Of course, Grace – through her insider's knowledge of Matron's sweet tooth – had played a vital part in the planning for the day.

The previous week, Ellie had been talking to Sanjay about the fact that the hospital was all of England he had ever seen. She had remarked idly that she was enjoying getting to know Brighton in her rare spare moments, and would love to show him around one day. He had seized upon the idea at once. Initially, Ellie had laughed him off, but the more she had thought about it, the more the idea of strolling round the city and along the pier with him had grown and grown in her mind, until she couldn't bear the thought of it not happening. Sanjay's strength and mobility were increasing day by day; in many ways, Ellie had reasoned with herself, this was merely a natural extension of their walks in the hospital gardens.

But as caught up in the scheme as she was, Ellie suspected that she would have work to do to convince her superiors. And this was where Grace's input had proved invaluable.

"Don't bother with old sourpuss Sister Adam," she had advised Ellie. "I'd go straight to Matron. I know she seems like a bit of a battle axe, but she's actually very reasonable. She only wants what's best for the patients and the hospital; I can't see her objecting to you using your free time for something like this. Besides, if he had family or friends in the country, she might be allowing him out for short spells with them at this stage. Yes, Matron's definitely your best bet. But it wouldn't hurt to take her a bag of lemon drops just to sweeten her up, so to speak. They're her favourites."

And so Ellie had done just that – though such sweet treats were becoming harder to get hold of – and had found that Grace was right. Matron was amenable to the plan, though hadn't agreed to it without Ellie submitting to a long and detailed list of rules first. As the list drew to a close, Ellie had glanced again at the photograph on the matron's desk. Feeling buoyed up with the success of her mission, she asked: "Is that your son?"

Matron looked slowly towards the photograph, as though surprised to find it there. "Yes," she said slowly. "Gregory."

"Is he serving in France?"

"He's missing," Matron said gruffly. "Missing in action. There's been no word for months."

Ellie felt her smile slide from her face. "Matron, I. . ."

"Now, girl, none of your silliness. You just take good care of that soldier, and see that he has a nice day."

"Yes, Matron."

Sister Adam, predictably, had been furious. Ellie had put off telling her until the last possible moment. She couldn't overrule Matron, of course, but Ellie suspected that the older nurse would find ways to punish her nonetheless.

"It's a beautiful day for it today too," Grace was saying, dabbing powder on her nose, as Ellie ran a

106

comb through her hair, then tied it back with a ribbon. "I say, would you like to borrow my cardigan?" she added, proffering the beautiful duckling-coloured garment she had just removed.

"Oh," Ellie said, staring longingly at the soft wool, "it's all right. I have a cardigan. But thank you."

"Hmmm, yes," said Grace, eyeing Ellie's plain and somewhat worn cardigan. "But it's always nice to wear something pretty for your afternoon off."

"Well. . ."

"Oh, go on," she said, and was draping the cardigan over Ellie's shoulders before she could utter more half-hearted protests. "There!" she proclaimed, stepping back as Ellie slid her arms into the sleeves. "It's just the colour for a beautiful spring day. Private Das is a lucky gent to have a lovely girl like you on his arm." She gave a wink and then was gone, before Ellie could object to this interpretation of her day's plans.

Ellie took one more glance in the mirror, blowing a strand of hair that had already broken free of the ribbon out of her face. Why was everyone acting as though there were something romantic about this outing? Aunt Frances had been just the same last night, teasing Ellie about her "stepping out" with a "handsome soldier".

It's just like walking in the gardens, she told herself once more. *That's all.*

But her stomach fluttered and twitched as she made her way to her ward to collect Sanjay. *It's just because everyone else has made such a fuss*, she thought. *It's their fault I feel all shy now.*

She was glad to see that Sister Adam wasn't in the ward. Grace was leaning over Corporal Snow, and glanced up as Ellie walked in. She looked pointedly in the direction of Sanjay, dressed in a clean uniform and sitting on the edge of his bed, grinned broadly and then went back to her work.

Ellie marched quickly over to Sanjay's bed. He tilted his head to one side quizzically when he saw her expression.

"Why do you look so cross?" he asked softly.

"What? I don't!" Ellie said, trying to force her forehead and jaw to relax.

He laughed and she felt her smile spreading across her face. "It's nice to see you not in your uniform," he said.

Ellie glanced at him, waiting to see if he would say more, but he merely looked calmly back at her, a smile still playing at the edge of his mouth.

"Thank you," she replied, then blushed furiously. That wasn't the right response. "It's nice to see you actually dressed for a change," she said next, going on the attack to disguise her embarrassment.

It was true that she'd only ever seen Sanjay in hospital pyjamas, with his dressing gown on top when they went for walks. He looked so smart in his uniform, with his hair neatly combed.

"Well, then," he said, a teasing note in his voice, "shall we go or are we going to sit here in our nice clothes with Sister Adam all afternoon?"

"Lord, no!" Ellie grinned, holding out her hand to help him stand. When upright, he picked up his walking stick with his right hand and offered her his left arm. She took it, even though they both knew that it would be her supporting him, really.

As they walked towards the door, Private Pope let out a shrill whistle and Corporal Snow called out, "Have a wonderful afternoon, the pair of you." The other soldiers and Grace were grinning at them, although Private Brown wore a hint of a frown as he said, "You make sure you take care of our Nurse Phillips, Private."

Again, Ellie felt her cheeks burning and – for one shameful moment – wished Sanjay would walk faster so that they could escape. But he looked unruffled; he merely smiled and nodded his head, lifting a couple of fingers from the head of his walking stick to offer them a lazy wave.

Having finally completed their escape from the hospital, Ellie wanted to spare Sanjay's leg too much strain, so they caught a tram down to the seafront. The people of Brighton were accustomed to seeing Indian soldiers, but Ellie noticed that Sanjay still drew a lot of attention – perhaps as a result of accompanying a young English girl. One little copper-haired girl on the tram stared and stared at him, until her mother whispered in her ear and she looked hastily away.

"That's all right," Sanjay said, leaning forward to address the mother. "I am fascinated too; I have not seen many little girls with such a beautiful colour hair."

The girl beamed and her mother smiled gratefully. "Thank you, sir. And thank you for all you've done in France too."

A few other passengers around them murmured their agreement. Ellie looked around in astonishment, but as ever, Sanjay took it in his stride. One old man did shake his head, but to this both Ellie and Sanjay affected obliviousness.

So, too, was he relaxed about the crowds of people as they alighted from the tram at the Palace Pier.

"My dear Eleanor," he said, chuckling as she cast around wildly for a way through the scrum, "compared to Delhi, this is as calm as the hospital gardens!"

She led him out on to the pier and they strolled the length of it. The day was still fine and they enjoyed the feel of the sea spray on their faces. When they reached the end, they turned to face back towards the city, and Ellie pointed out the landmarks that she knew.

"And, of course, in the other direction there's nothing really until you hit France."

Sanjay shuddered. "Please, don't speak of that place. I see it in my nightmares enough as it is."

"Sorry," Ellie said, patting his arm. "Truly, I am.

It's so strange; I always longed to go to France, but now. . ."

"What are those birds?" Sanjay asked now, gesturing towards the seagulls that swooped and called, hoping for some offerings from a tourist's picnic lunch. "I saw them on the boat coming over here before we were shipped to France. And then again on the journey back after I was injured. They're one of the only things I truly remember from that awful journey."

It was Ellie's turn to shiver, thinking of how injured he had been; how unwell and disoriented and frightened he must have felt. "Seagulls," she replied, trying to distract them both from the memory. "Those big ones are gannets. Don't you have them in India?"

"*Sea*gulls? So they are sea birds, yes? Well, Delhi is inland, so no, not there."

Of course, Ellie knew that; she had studied maps of India since becoming friends with Sanjay. Why did she always act like such a dunce around him?

"Do you know," Sanjay was saying now, drawing her attention back to him, "before I was sent to France with the army, I had never seen the sea! The journey over from India was quite a shock, I can tell you.

Across the Arabian Sea, around the coast of Africa and into the Mediterranean through the Suez Canal."

'Really?" Ellie said, glad of the change of subject, her mind a-glitter with the thought of this journey, of the things he had seen. "I have lived by the sea all my life. Just always the same bit of sea up until now."

"Of course," he replied. "In the famous Endstone before you came to Brighton."

"Yes." Ellie smiled. He overemphasized the *stone* in Endstone, but despite always feeling at such a disadvantage with him, she couldn't bring herself to correct him. His English – a second language – was so close to flawless. And she loved the subtle flavours of his accent, reminding her that in some ways where he came from might as well have been another world.

As they walked back towards the seafront, they stopped at a Punch and Judy show and laughed as they watched the puppets clobbering each other.

"You know," Sanjay murmured, leaning towards her ear, "that female puppet reminds me of Matron when someone has riled her."

Ellie had to press her handkerchief to her mouth to conceal her unladylike spluttering.

They sat on a bench back at the seafront. Sanjay had wanted to walk on the beach but Ellie had thought he might struggle on the shingle with his walking stick, so they agreed on this compromise.

"Why did you join the army?" Ellie asked him now. Conscription had been introduced only recently in England, but she knew it didn't exist in India.

"Well, first and foremost it was about money," Sanjay said frankly. Ellie thought of how her mother would have squirmed to hear him speak so openly on the subject. "My family are not wealthy and as the oldest son, I knew I must start earning money as soon as possible. The pay in the Indian army is good – better than you can earn in most other professions there. It seemed the best chance I had to save up enough money that I could eventually continue my studies to be a doctor, while helping to support my family. Also, there are some in India who believe that if we support the British through this war, we will be in a stronger position to win independence for our country afterwards."

"Independence?" Ellie repeated.

"Well, yes, Ellie," Sanjay said, with a touch of

impatience. "You must know that, for us, there is no reason for our country to be governed by yours."

The truth was that Ellie hadn't really given it much thought, though she knew better than to voice that aloud. She supposed, now that she did come to think of it, there *was* no reason – at least, no reason from the Indians' perspective. Suspecting they had strayed into conversational territory that could only lead to her feeling and sounding silly in front of Sanjay, she steered them away, promising herself she would read more about Indian history before they spoke of it again.

"And so you joined the army, even though you knew it would mean fighting in the war?"

"Well, yes, of course. By the time I joined, the war had started and we were already involved. But boys, you know, boys always think they are born soldiers. Until they have to fight in reality. Such foolishness. . ."

"But you *will* continue your studies?"

"Certainly," he said. He had such confidence in everything he said and did. There had been a time, Ellie knew, when the doctors had thought they might have to amputate his leg. Ellie wondered whether any part of him had believed that was really a possibility.

"I will be the first doctor in the family," he was saying now, the same note of pride in his voice.

"Well, Dr Das," said Ellie, shaking her thoughts off like droplets of water, "how would you feel about stopping into one of those nice seaside tearooms?"

"Tea." Sanjay smiled. "That is one thing that is the same here as at home; everybody drinks tea all day long!"

"Really?" Ellie said, as they strolled together towards a tearoom that she had spotted earlier. She hoarded these titbits – things that Sanjay said were similar between his country and her own – like a magpie gathering sparkly objects to pore over when she was by herself.

"And what about you, Nurse Phillips?" Sanjay asked now. "What made you decide to be a nurse? You're still so young."

"I'm not so much younger than you!" Ellie said hotly.

He laughed as they walked into the tearoom and were shown to a table by the window. Once again, Ellie was aware of the eyes of the other customers tracking their movements, as well as some raised eyebrows and muttered conversation. If Sanjay noticed, he did not seem to be bothered by it.

"I know you're not," he went on once they were settled into their seats. "But you are younger than any of the other nurses at the hospital."

"It's true," Ellie said. "They don't usually accept voluntary nurses as young as me. In fact, I think Matron had to fudge things a bit with the paperwork to make it possible."

"You are a prodigy, is that it?" he asked, his tone serious but his eyes dancing.

"No, no," Ellie said hurriedly, feeling flushed and flustered. "Nothing like that. My father was the doctor in Endstone. I always took an interest in what he did and when I was older I helped out in the surgery. Just with paperwork, usually, things like that." Ellie felt Sanjay's steady gaze on her and read the gentle question in his eyes. "He was killed in the war," she said, pleased to note that she was able to say it without her voice wobbling now.

"I'm very sorry to hear that, Ellie," he said. And he sounded it.

They broke off their conversation to order. Sanjay

said he was in Ellie's hands so she ordered tea for two, and two slices of Victoria sponge cake.

"It's my absolute favourite," she said, as the waitress bustled off. "I haven't had it in an age, what with supplies being somewhat scarce these days. I'm surprised to see it on the menu, so we mustn't pass up the opportunity.

"Anyway," she went on, "when Father went away to war, his young apprentice Thomas took over in the surgery, and I helped him too, where I could. But then Father was killed, and a Belgian doctor arrived with his family. At first . . . I don't know. . . I suppose I didn't like the idea of anyone trying to fill Father's shoes. It was a while before I would accept that he is a good doctor too. And the village needs him. . ."

"But you did accept it," Sanjay prompted.

"Yes," Ellie said. "I did. He's a wonderful man and a good doctor. Dr Mertens and Thomas taught me a lot. I suppose I've cared for my mother – she's never terribly well – and Charlie for a long time too. And then after the explosion at the factory. . ."

Sanjay's dark eyes looked as big as dinner plates. Ellie waited while the waitress set down the teapot and cups in their dainty saucers, the plates with their slabs of fluffy sponge, cream and jam, the milk jugs, tea strainers and the little forks between them.

As the waitress walked off, she continued. "I was working in the munitions factory last year. There was a terrible explosion. Many people were very badly hurt and it caused a lot of damage. My friend Jack—"

"Jack?"

"Yes." Ellie busied herself pouring the tea. "He's . . . he's a very old friend. I've known him all my life, really. Well, he was hurt. His leg too, actually." Her eyes flickered up to Sanjay's, and then back to the teapot. "I took care of him until the doctors were able to. And then a bit afterwards, when he was recovering. I think after that I knew I wanted to be a nurse." She smiled. "Jack says I was the last one in the village to work that out."

"It sounds as though this Jack knows you very well."

Ellie shifted in her seat, toying with her slice of cake. "Well, yes, like I say, we're very old friends. . ."

Friends? she thought. *That's not all.* But a conversation with one of her patients was hardly the place to go into all that, she told herself crossly.

Their talk moved on to the medical profession in their two countries.

"It is pleasing to me that, in this country, women have access to medical education. I'm sorry to say that it is not the case in mine."

"Well, yes," said Ellie. "But look at our hospital. There is not a single female doctor there."

"Not yet," said Sanjay, smiling at her as he held his teacup with surprising delicacy. "Not now. But there will be. After your Mrs Garrett Anderson – Dr Garrett Anderson, I should say – it is only a matter of time before it becomes more widespread. And in my country too. I am sure of it."

Now here was a topic Ellie knew all about; Elizabeth Garrett Anderson had been the first English woman to qualify as a physician and surgeon, though she had had to battle her way through. She and Sanjay chatted comfortably about this incredible woman for a while, before Ellie realized with a start how late it was getting.

They hurried – as much as Sanjay's leg would allow them – back to the hospital, giggling together about how grumpy Sister Adam must have been by the time her shift finished. Ellie liked to see this less serious, more mischievous side to her new friend.

She left him at the doors to the hospital. "If Matron sees me she might decide to be cross with me after all!"

He laughed, a rich, musical sound. "Thank you, Nurse Phillips, for a wonderful afternoon." He took her hand and brushed his lips lightly against it.

"Oh, I'm Nurse Phillips again, am I?" she joked, trying to disguise her reaction to the kiss.

He merely smiled. "Goodnight, Nurse Phillips. I will see you tomorrow."

"Goodnight," she replied. After seeing him safely through the doors, she scampered off in the direction of home, her cheeks still flaming. Thank goodness Aunt Frances hadn't been there to see that!

Tucked up in bed, she replayed the events of the day; the details of every conversation, the way his laughter seemed to catch Sanjay by surprise, how much she loved being the cause of it. . . It was only as she was drifting off to sleep that she realized she had once again forgotten to write to Jack.

NINE

JUNE

Ellie rested the back of her hand against Private Garrett's forehead and was relieved to find it a little cooler. A week previously he had contracted a nasty chest infection and he was only just emerging on the other side of it. Such an infection was hardly surprising, given the damage inflicted to his lungs by gas in the trenches, not to mention his generally poor health, but in his weakened state, there was every chance that it might prove fatal. They had all been very worried.

The extra time and attention that the private had needed, added to an influx of new and – in many cases – terribly injured patients to the hospital the previous weekend, meant that the staff had been working longer and longer hours in a bid to try to keep on top of it all. Ellie felt her tiredness down to her very bones; her organs, she felt sure, were working at a slower pace, like factory machinery that needed replacement parts.

As she refilled Private Garrett's water glass from the jug, listening to his painfully shallow breathing, she felt her body slump slightly against the side of his bed.

"Nurse Phillips!"

Sister Adam's harsh voice felt like a wire brush on her tender nerves. She straightened herself up with effort and turned to meet the ward sister in the centre of the room.

"Nurse Phillips," she said again, "your cap is not at the correct angle. I could see that all the way from here. How you managed not to notice it in the mirror this morning is a mystery to me."

Ellie's nails dug into her palms. *I managed not to notice it because it is five hours since I left the house this morning,* she thought, *and I certainly didn't have time to look in the mirror before I did so. Because I have been clambering around under beds and dashing in and out of store cupboards since then, and I haven't even had the chance to go to visit the lavatory. Because it just* does not matter *anyway*.

She said none of this. Instead, through a jaw so tight she felt as though the words were having to flatten themselves to get out, she said, "I'm sorry, Sister Adam. Would you like me to go and see to it now?"

"Now? Goodness me, child, not now! We're all rushed off our feet here. We can't wait for you while you primp in front of the mirror! Just make sure you are neater tomorrow, or I shall have to speak with Matron."

It was a good thing that the sister now swept away, smirking down her nose, for Ellie could barely contain her reaction to the hated term "child". The first time the sister had ever addressed her this way, she had made the mistake of flinching and it had not gone unnoticed. This time she stood, immobilized by anger, a wave of white hot rage pouring down her spine like molten metal. She couldn't go to the washroom to calm down – Sister Adam had just forbidden her. Before the ward sister could turn round and berate her for idling, she spun on her heel and stormed over to Sanjay's corner.

As she approached, she saw that he was grinning; he had clearly overheard the whole exchange. But on seeing her face, his own grew serious.

"Nurse Phillips," he said in a clear tone, "might I trouble you for a glass of water too, please?"

Ellie couldn't trust herself to reply, but reached for the trolley and poured him one with shaking hands.

"Take some deep breaths," he muttered to her softly, as she handed him the glass. "Do not let her get the better of you; that is what she wants."

"She . . . she. . . I can't. . ."

"Sssh," he said soothingly, "you can. You know you are a better person than she is. You know she only behaves this way because she is envious of you – of the responsibilities you have been given so young, of how well liked you are."

Ellie closed her eyes and sucked in some wobbly breaths. His voice was so soft, so calm, so confident; she felt the pain receding from her forehead, the burning sensation from behind her eyes.

"I can't just let her treat me this way and not do anything about it. . ."

She felt his hand on her elbow and opened her

eyes. His grin was so surprising, so mischievous, she couldn't help but mimic it.

"I quite agree. But you must know the expression 'revenge is a dish best served cold'."

"Well, yes, but. . ."

"So, cool down. We will speak more later. Now, go and carry on with your tasks before she finds another excuse to reprimand you."

Ellie nodded and gave him a small but grateful smile.

As she walked across the room towards Private Pope, Sister Adam called to her again.

"Oh, and Nurse Phillips?" Ellie could almost feel her hair standing on end, almost hear a growl forming in the back of her throat like a wild animal. "Are these beds really the correct distance from the wall? I think if I were to take out my handkerchief I would discover that they are not. Just because we are busy, that is no reason for standards to slip."

Ellie huffed a breath out through her nose and continued on her way. As she reached Private Pope's bed, she glanced back at Sanjay. He was grinning broadly as if Sister Adam had just made the best joke

126

he had ever heard. As he caught her eye, he slowly and deliberately mouthed the word "cold".

"All right, everyone," Ellie called softly. "Sister Adam has gone on her break. We've got half an hour until she comes back, so let's hurry."

It was the following day and she and Sanjay had come up with their plan. The other men on the ward had been only too happy to get involved; everyone was tired of the ward sister and her nagging ways. Corporal Snow had been a little anxious at first, but once he was reassured that nobody would be hurt or treated unkindly, he soon joined in.

"Just the kind of high jinks the young lads sometimes get up to during training," he said through a chuckle now, as Ellie and Grace each took a corner of his bed, and wheeled it into the centre of the ward.

Like the corporal, Grace had been unsure about getting involved. Ellie had understood; no one wanted to draw unfavourable attention to themselves. But in the end, she couldn't resist joining in the plotting, and now, it seemed, in the execution of the plan.

The men who were stronger and more mobile –

including Sanjay these days – were also helping. Before long, all twelve beds were pushed together in the centre of the room, forming one massive rectangular bed.

"Quickly, everyone back into his own bed," Ellie said now, and the men who had been up hurried to comply, breaking down into helpless laughter as they clambered over one another to get into position.

Grace was doubled up with giggles already, tears pouring down her face, but though she was grinning too, Ellie felt a fluttering in her guts. When Sister Adam came in, she wanted everyone to behave as though nothing out of the ordinary were going on, but the longer she had to wait for her own performance, the more nervous she felt about it.

"Oh, I can't. . ." Grace gasped, "I have to go and wash my face. . ." She staggered from the room, hands pressed against her ribs.

Ellie walked round to Sanjay's bed, at the back left of the big rectangle. He alone was sitting calmly, only the smallest smile playing on his lips.

"Go on with your tasks," he said to her quietly. "It will help you to feel more at ease."

She nodded and went over to fetch the dressing trolley from the front corner of the room. She was restocking it, her back to the door, when she heard the sharp rap of shoes against the tiled floor. Trying desperately to keep her posture natural, Ellie continued piling bandages on to the trolley. She heard the footsteps stop, followed by a sharp inhalation of breath, which seemed to echo in the quiet of the room.

"What. . ." Sister Adam hissed. "What is the meaning of this?"

Ellie turned around slowly to face the older woman, who stood frozen in the doorway, her neck a flaming red colour. Ellie watched in fascination as the colour slowly bled upwards and into her face.

"Sister Adam?" she said, her voice gratifyingly calm, though her heartbeat thundered in her ears. "Is everything all right?"

The ward sister swung round to look at her, her movements jerky, her eyes wild. "What have you *done*?" she squawked.

Ellie shook her head slowly. "Done? I . . . I don't understand."

There was a snorting sound from the centre of the room. Ellie glanced towards the giant bed and saw that Private Pope had his hands stuffed against his mouth, but that this was doing nothing to stop his shoulders from shaking. Beside him, Private Brown had his lips pressed firmly together. Sanjay was calmly turning the pages of his newspaper, as though nothing in the least bit out of the ordinary were occurring.

"Fix it!" Sister Adam hissed, lurching towards the cluster of beds, and yanking at the end of Sergeant Bateman's bed, as he stared studiously at his crossword. The castors were all facing different directions, so the bed scarcely moved at all; instead the sister staggered backwards with the force of her attempt.

Private Brown was now emitting a high-pitched sound as he leaned towards his friend in the neighbouring bed. With a cry of rage, Sister Adam dropped to her knees, scrabbling around under the bed to turn the castors.

As she emerged, Ellie said, her voice clear and even, "Oh, Sister Adam, your cap is a little askew. Here, let me—"

But she didn't get any further. As though this had been a cue, Private Brown's laughter finally broke free in a shout, and then they were all lost. Even Private Garrett was panting wheezily, his eyes streaming.

The sister's face was now a deep purple colour. She stepped towards Ellie, a look of pure hatred in her eyes. "You. . ."

She didn't finish the thought; instead she turned and ran from the ward. Grace was just coming back in. One glance at Sister Adam's face and she fled back to the washroom, peals of musical laughter streaming behind her.

Ellie's own control abandoned her and she tottered over to Sanjay's bed, her breath coming in sobbing sounds. Sanjay appeared calm, though his smile seemed to give off a light all by itself.

Ellie was feeling the first flickers of conscience, but she hadn't stopped laughing as she collapsed, sitting next to him on the bed and leaning her forehead forward towards his pillow. He patted her on the back. She could hear the smile still in his voice as he said, "That was very well done. I think maybe you should abandon nursing for a career on the stage."

"Don't," Ellie moaned, pressing a hand to her stomach, whose muscles were protesting.

"Ellie?" The voice was so unexpected that for a moment she didn't recognize it, thought she had imagined it in the cacophony of laughter all around her. She sat up slowly, feeling Sanjay's hand still firm against her back, and turned towards the end of the bed, which was pressed in turn against the end of Private Pope's bed. Standing beside the young private's oblivious head was Jack.

Ellie's cheeks were still stretched painfully in a smile as she stared stupidly at him, trying to make sense of his presence. Jack's face showed the very last ripples of his own smile, giving way to confusion.

"Jack," she said slowly, as she wiped her eyes with the back of her hand. "Jack! What are you doing here?" She slid off the bed and took a step towards him.

"I came to see you. . ." he said, equally slowly.

She noticed that he was clasping a bunch of yellow horned poppies, which grew on the clifftops of Endstone at this time of year. She took another step towards him, though he showed no sign of moving.

"Why didn't you tell me you were coming?" she asked.

"I. . . I . . ." He looked like someone slowly waking up. "Would it have made a difference if I had?" His eyebrows moving towards each other. "You've barely been writing at all these last months. I haven't heard from you for weeks. I was worried." She heard an unfamiliar, harsh note creep into his voice. "I see now you have been terribly busy with your important nursing work." His eyes looked past her, towards Sanjay.

"Jack," she said, an icy cold feeling slipping into her stomach. She moved quickly to his side, taking his elbow. "Jack, I'm sorry. . . I *have* been busy, it's just—"

"*Nurse* Phillips!"

Ellie closed her eyes for a moment, before turning to face the doorway, where Matron stood, flanked by a murderous-looking Sister Adam.

"Come here at once! And you, young man!"

Ellie and Jack obeyed, hurrying to the entrance to the ward.

"Against my better judgment, I allowed myself to be persuaded to permit this young gentleman to come and see you on the ward." Ellie knew well how persuasive Jack could be. She imagined his charming smile and felt a pang to see how far he was from smiling now.

"I can see that I have been very much mistaken about you, Nurse Phillips." Ellie looked at the floor. "Young man, you will have to leave at once. Nurse Phillips, I will see you in my office in two minutes."

As Matron stalked from the room, Ellie turned to Jack and seized his hand, ignoring Sister Adam who still hovered threateningly beside her.

"Jack, I finish at six. Please, please, will you come to our digs for tea?"

He wouldn't even look at her. "I have to get back to Endstone today. . ."

"Please, you can't go without us seeing each other properly. . ."

"You'd better not keep Matron waiting," the ward sister said with a sneer.

"*Please*, Jack!"

"All right," he said at last, pulling his hand back. "I'll see you back at your digs at half past six."

For once, Ellie and Frances had finished work at the same time, and were walking home together. But Ellie was not glad of it.

"Goodness knows, I don't like Phyllis Adam any

more than you do," Frances said gently, as they walked through the bright and bustling streets. "But when you react to her in that way, you only let yourself down."

"I know," Ellie said through clenched teeth. Matron had given her a thorough and humiliating dressing-down, the worst part of which had been that Ellie couldn't disagree with a single thing she had said. Matron had also made it very clear that the next time Ellie put a foot out of line, she would find herself on her way back to Endstone for good. She felt small and stupid, and very weary. All she wanted to do was to pull a blanket over her head and sleep it all away.

"Don't forget you are a professional, Ellie," Frances said, looking as though it hurt her to have to speak to her niece this way. "And a grown-up. You're not at school or messing around at home with Jack."

Ellie winced at the mention of Jack. "I *know*," she said again. She had told her aunt that Jack was coming round for tea.

"I don't want to lecture you, Ellie. I know how hard you work, and that I don't have to remind you how important our job is. Just. . ." She took a deep breath. "Just, remember that I helped to convince

Matron to take you on – to put herself on the line by accepting such a young voluntary nurse – and your actions reflect on me too."

They were at the door to their digs now, and Ellie closed her eyes as Frances put her key into the lock, feeling her aunt's last words like a punch in her stomach. "I'm sorry," she whispered.

"Come on," Aunt Frances said kindly, and Ellie opened her eyes and followed her in. "Why don't you go and change before Jack gets here?"

Ellie obeyed mechanically, and was sitting on her bed in her skirt and blouse, staring into space, when she heard the knock at the front door ten minutes later.

Jack and Frances were sitting at the kitchen table with the teapot between them when she walked in. Her aunt was still in her uniform. Ellie noticed distractedly that there was no sign of the flowers from earlier.

"Ah, Ellie," Aunt Frances said warmly. "Will you pour while I go and change?"

Ellie nodded and sat down in front of Jack, pulling the teapot and three cups towards her.

"Did you have a nice day?" she asked Jack, feeling strangely shy.

"It was all right," he said a little stiffly. "Seems like a nice enough place, though it was a bit overwhelming, not knowing anywhere or anyone. There are so many people!"

"I know," Ellie agreed. "I felt that way when I first came here too." She pushed his teacup towards him, then made a sound of frustration. This was Jack; she couldn't make small talk with him! "Look, Jack, I'm so sorry I haven't been writing. The hours at the hospital are so long, and then when I get home I usually go more or less straight to bed. And then the longer I leave it, the more I have to tell you about, so I just . . . don't. That's no excuse, I know. . ."

"It certainly seemed like you were busy today," he replied. His tone was even and he smiled as he said it, but it wasn't his usual smile. There was no warmth to it, though Ellie could see that he was trying hard to be as normal as possible.

"That's not what it's usually like!" she protested. "I've told you about Sister Adam, and—"

"Ellie, you don't have to explain anything to me—"

137

"Of course I do! You're my best friend—"

"*Friends*. . ."

"Jack—"

"It just seems to me you're forgetting all about Endstone, about your family. About me. . . Maybe that's as it should be—"

"I'm not forgetting anything—"

"Jack," Frances said, having reentered the room unnoticed. "Don't be upset. No, really," she went on as he made a dismissive noise, "it's understandable that you are. Ellie knows what it's like to be the one who's left behind. But *you* know what it's like to be caught up in your work when you're doing something so important—"

"I don't need you to speak for me!" Ellie cried, leaping to her feet.

There was a moment of stunned silence. "Of course you don't," Frances replied softly.

Ellie couldn't bear the way her aunt and Jack were looking at her; as though she were a complete stranger. She sank miserably back into her seat. "I'm sorry," she said again, but she knew she didn't sound it. "I'm sorry, sorry, sorry to everyone!"

"Ellie—" Frances began.

"I should go," Jack said suddenly.

Ellie looked up at him, feeling tears spring to her eyes. "You've only just got here."

"It's getting late, and I'm working tomorrow. I should really get the half-past-seven train."

"I'll walk you to the station."

"No," he said, then softened his tone with visible effort. "No, it's fine. You're tired. You've got work tomorrow too. I'm a big boy," he said, with another smile that didn't reach his eyes. "You stay here, have your dinner and then try to get some rest. I'll see you. . . Goodbye, Miss Phillips," he said, nodding to Aunt Frances.

Ellie's aunt looked stricken as she followed him to the door. Ellie couldn't move. She sat frozen in her seat, staring after them both.

TEN

MID JUNE

"Make sure you get right into the corners with that broom, Phillips," Sister Adam said, one morning in mid June. "I wouldn't want to have to complain to Matron about you slacking again."

Ellie would have happily fed Charlie from any inch of the ward floor, so confident was she of its spotlessness – not to mention her deep scepticism regarding the ward sister's reluctance to run to Matron with stories – but all she said was, "Yes, Sister. I'll go over it again."

Since their prank over a week ago, Sister Adam had been worse than ever, as though determined to recover her lost dignity with outright tyranny. In particular, she liked to remind Ellie how easily she could have her sent home at any time. Ellie no longer felt tempted to argue back; it would only make things worse. She had resolved to keep her head down and work as hard as she could. She had wanted this job so much; she wasn't going to allow herself to throw it away. Besides, immersing herself more than ever in her work took her mind off Jack, whom she hadn't heard from since he had come to Brighton.

"And then collect the bedpans," Sister Adam was saying now. "And do try to move a bit quicker."

"Yes, Sister," Ellie said again.

Retracing her steps with the broom, she approached Sanjay's bed just as Dr Curtis was concluding his daily check-up.

"All in all, Private Das," she heard him say, "I am delighted with your recovery. Your leg has healed more satisfactorily than I had ever dared to hope. Another week or so of rest and increasing the amount of walking you do every day, and you should be ready to be shipped back out."

Ellie struggled to hear Sanjay's response over her own breathing, which was suddenly strangely noisy.

"Thank you, Doctor," Sanjay replied quietly. "That is welcome news indeed."

"Very good, very good. I'll see you tomorrow."

As the doctor walked away, scribbling something in his notes, Ellie approached Sanjay's side, painting a smile on to her face that felt more like a grimace.

"Great news!" she said, reaching under the bed with her broom, so that Sister Adam couldn't object if she chose that moment to look round. "You're as good as new, almost!"

"Yes," Sanjay said, his dark eyes lowered, reminding Ellie of when she had first known him; when he wouldn't even meet her eye. It felt like another lifetime. "It will be good to feel whole again." He looked up briefly, and gave her a small smile, but it was like the tiniest glimmer of sunlight on a wintry day compared to his normal dazzler.

Stop being so selfish, Ellie thought to herself, as she continued her sweeping. *You knew he was getting better, getting stronger; you wanted that. What did you think would happen when he did? It's your job to help people recover!*

She began collecting the bedpans and replacing

them with fresh ones. She couldn't help herself from glancing over to Sanjay's corner every few seconds, though. He was staring at his book, but he didn't seem to be turning the pages. She tried to imagine the bed empty, or another soldier in it – she had seen many others come and go by now – but quickly pushed the thought away as her eyes began to sting.

What's wrong with you? she asked herself impatiently. She tried to tell herself it was just concern over him returning to the trenches, especially after hearing how he had hated it there before, but she knew there was more to it.

She couldn't stop thinking about it all day.

I'll never see him again. The thought sprang unbidden to her mind that afternoon. It was so obvious. How could it still feel so shocking? *He'll go, and then I'll never see him again*. She found herself standing frozen in the middle of the ward, waiting for her breathing to normalize, a pile of bed linen in her outstretched arms.

She was still there when Frances suddenly dashed in, her face grey. "Ellie!" she said, removing the linen from her and placing it down, before seizing her niece by the hands. "Ellie. . . Something very bad has happened."

Ellie looked at her blankly, caught in her own thoughts, not even registering how strange it was to see her aunt upstairs in the hospital.

"Ellie, listen to me. Are you listening? We have to go. Jack has just telephoned from the Endstone surgery." Aunt Frances's words felt as though they were trickling too slowly into Ellie's ears to be understood. Frances paused, squeezing Ellie's hands. "Your mother and Charlie are fine—"

At last Ellie was shocked into alertness. "What? What do you mean? What's happened? Tell me, quickly!"

Frances complied. "There's been a bomb, in Endstone. An air raid. They're fine, Ellie," Frances went on hurriedly, as her niece staggered. "Josephine and Charlie are fine."

Grace had appeared by Ellie's side without her noticing. "Sit down," she said now, her arm around Ellie's back as she pushed her, resisting, into a chair.

"Jack!" Ellie said, trying to get back to her feet.

Grace pressed down firmly on Ellie's shoulders. Frances knelt in front of her, her hands shaking as they rested in Ellie's lap. "He's . . . he's safe too. He

144

was the one to call, remember? But, Ellie . . . his sister, and little George. . . They've been hurt. A lot of people have been hurt." She squeezed her eyes shut. "And Sarah Pritchard has been killed."

Ellie suddenly felt as though the floor were rushing towards her. Grace eased her head down between her knees, making soothing sounds, as Ellie sucked in deep breaths.

"What on earth . . . ?" she heard Grace saying, as her hand moved up and down Ellie's back. "Endstone is just a little civilian village, isn't it? What do the Germans want dropping bombs there?"

"I don't know," Frances was saying. She sounded close to tears. The only time Ellie had seen her aunt cry was when her father had died. She felt a rush of nausea rising up her throat and pressed the back of her hand to her mouth.

"Ellie," Frances was saying now, "I'm sorry, I'm so sorry, I know this is shocking. . . But we have to go. At once."

Ellie looked up and nodded, her hand still at her mouth. Of course they must. "Jack. . . Did he sound. . . Is he. . . ?"

"He's very worried, of course he is. He's probably in shock himself. But he's all right. Now, listen. I'll speak to Matron and tell her we're both needed there, in Endstone. I know she'll understand." Frances took a deep breath and set her mouth. "Then we should go back to the digs, pack our bags and get on a train as soon as possible. This is important. We are going to have to be strong now, Ellie."

Ellie nodded again as Grace pressed a glass of water into her hands. In her peripheral vision, Ellie could feel the concerned eyes of the men she had come to know so well, but it felt as though they were on the other side of a pane of glass.

She thought of her village, and was surprised at how unfamiliar it was; as though Endstone hadn't been in her mind for weeks. She pictured the square; the church, the store, the fountain, the pub; the woods, with Father's things buried beneath their favourite oak tree; the clifftops and the beaches. Her home. She thought of all the people there, people she had known her whole life. Anna and George Scott. . . Thomas and his new wife, Sarah, who had been married for less than a year. . . Her family. Jack.

He had been right. She had been so caught up in her life in Brighton, it was as though she had forgotten it all. And now it had almost been taken from her.

She drew herself up and took hold of her aunt's clammy hand again. "You're right. We should go at once."

ELEVEN

LATER THAT DAY

Ellie and Frances leaped off the train as soon as it came to a halt in Endstone station, their bags in their hands. It was early evening and the sky was still bright, but even from several miles away, they had been able to see the big cloud of smoke over the village. Ellie's bicycle was up at her house, where Jack had returned it after her last visit all those months ago, so they hurried on foot into the village.

Jack had called Frances within a couple of hours of the bomb, as soon as he had seen how bad the situation was. He had told her that ambulances had been sent for from Canterbury to help with the most seriously injured. But Endstone wasn't the only place that had been hit. They hadn't been able to say for sure when they'd be able to get there. With the two doctors still reeling from the loss of Sarah Pritchard, the need for Ellie and Frances's help was very real.

"Should we go to the surgery, do you think?" Frances asked Ellie breathlessly, as they jogged along the path.

"Not if there were about a dozen injured, as you said," Ellie replied. "There wouldn't be room for them all there."

"Then where do you think. . . ?"

"The church," Ellie said firmly. "It's the biggest space, and surely where people will have gathered, so we should be able to get more information there, at the very least."

"All right," Frances agreed, and they fell silent.

As they got closer to the square, the smoke became thicker. Ellie suddenly stumbled to a halt. "Oh. . ." she breathed.

The bomb had exploded just outside the village store, shattering the windows and those of the buildings around. Part of the façade had been ripped away too, leaving it looking ragged and strangely indecent. A network of cracks in the cobbles led from the store across the square to the fountain.

Frances took Ellie by the arm. "Come on," she said gently. "It seems as though you were right."

Sure enough, people were gathered by the church, in the grounds and doorway. There was Miss Smith, a teacher from the local school, and Ted Townsend, a local fisherman; Mrs Baxter and Mrs Dorling – two widowed sisters whom Ellie hadn't seen for months. Mr Berry, the postman, sat slumped against the wall, his head in his hands.

"Eleanor!" called Mrs Baxter as they walked towards her through the front graveyard. "Thank goodness you're here!"

Ellie smiled and offered a few words of greeting, then hurried on, desperate to get inside.

Jack was the first thing she saw as her eyes adjusted to the gloom. He was bustling through the vestibule, with arms full of bedding, reminding Ellie strangely of herself earlier that afternoon. Was it really still the same day?

"Jack!" she cried, and wrapped her arms around him, crushing the bedding between their bodies.

"Ellie," he murmured, his voice thick as he spoke into her hair. "Oh, Ellie. . ."

"Sssh, it's all right," she said soothingly. "We're here now. What do we need to do?"

He guided them into the main part of the church, where the pews had been pushed to the sides or turned into makeshift beds. Ellie could see some people lying on them; others rushed around, trying to help.

"How many. . . ?" she asked.

"Sarah's the only one. . ." Jack pressed the heels of his hands hard against his eyes. "Her father and Thomas are with the rest of the family. I haven't seen them for a few hours. There are twelve who've been hurt. Canterbury Hospital still haven't been able to send help; I've left Alice in the surgery in case they telephone back. Most of the injured are conscious, at least, but George. . ." His voice disappeared.

Ellie squeezed his arm. "Take us to him."

Jack nodded, and led them through the crush of people to a pew, on which his eleven-year-old brother George lay motionless. The boys' mother, Mabel, was kneeling before her son, pressing a white cloth to his head, which was already soaked through with red.

Their sister, Anna, sat on the pew beside him, her face blackened with smoke, her eyes staring, unfocused, ahead of her.

"Mam," Jack said gently, "Ellie's here now, Mam. She's going to patch Georgie up. Make space for her, Mam."

Mabel had been silent, but as she looked up at Ellie, she sucked in a gasping breath. "Oh my God, oh my God. . ." She began to sob.

Ellie took her hands, removing the bloody cloth from them. "Sssh, sssh. We're here. It's going to be all right."

Mabel's weeping only became louder. Frances too joined the crowd around George and peered at bleeding wound on his brow, brushing away some of his red-gold curls with her hand.

"Has he been unconscious ever since he was hurt?" she asked Jack.

"Not all the time," Jack replied, tears shimmering in his eyes as he looked down at his little brother. "He's been drifting in and out."

"He's probably concussed," Frances said decisively. "But the cut itself isn't deep. I don't think he'll need stitches. We have to try to keep him awake, though. Jack, can you go and get plenty of clean water?"

He nodded again, looking relieved to have been given something to do, and stumbled away, calling to some nearby boys to help him.

Mabel had begun to mutter. Ellie had to crane closer to hear what she was saying.

"How much more? How much more? My Will's already away; Joe's in prison. . ." Jack's father had been arrested and charged in connection with the explosion at the factory last year. "Jack injured, and now the other two. . . How much more. . . I can't. . ."

Her breath was coming quicker and quicker.

"She's hysterical," Frances said. She was now having a look at Anna; the girl was covered in bleeding scratches, presumably from the shattered glass at the store front, but her dazed look and unnaturally pale skin beneath the smoke grime were even more worrying. "We need to calm her down."

"I know. . ." Ellie said. She stared around at all the injured, with a mounting sense of panic. "Mabel," she said, raising her voice and taking the woman's face in her hands. "We need you to be calm now. George and

Anna need you. Can you do that for me? Can you take some deep breaths for me?"

Tears were still pouring down Mabel's face, but she looked at Ellie, and then she nodded, taking a few obedient breaths.

Jack had returned with the water. Along with the two young boys he had enlisted, Mr Berry was now in tow. "It's all cold water," he said. "Is that all right?"

"That's good," Ellie said to him. "But we'll need some boiled water too. Mr Berry, do you think you could arrange that for us?"

"Certainly, Ellie," he said, and waddled off purposely.

"Jack, I need you to try to keep your mother calm while Ellie looks after George," Frances said now. "I'm going to go around and look at the others who are injured; it's clear George is our priority but we have to work out where we're most needed after that. Ellie, see if you can get him awake and talking."

As Frances bustled off to look at the other casualties, Ellie took a seat beside George. First she washed her hands with the water, then she took a clean cloth, soaked it and pressed it against his head.

"George," she said in a loud voice. "George? Can you hear me, George?"

He made a small moaning sound as she moved the cloth against his wound, but otherwise didn't respond.

"George, I need you to wake up for me. Can you do that? George? George, you should see your big brother. I've never seen him so worried about anyone. If you open your eyes, you can see his silly face for yourself. George?"

"M . . . Mam," he croaked, eliciting a gasp from Mabel on the floor beside him. She scrabbled to his side and seized his hand, covering it with kisses.

"Good boy," Ellie said. She could see that the bleeding from his wound was already slowing; Frances was right, he wouldn't need stitches. "Good boy," she said again, pulling her bag towards her and drawing out some dressing. "You stay awake now."

"Mam. . ."

"I'm here, love. I'm here."

"Sleepy, Mam. . ."

"I know, love, but you have to stay awake," Mabel sobbed. "Ellie says so, and she knows what's what, doesn't she? She's a clever girl, our Ellie."

Ellie finished bandaging the wound, then gently sat George up.

"Mabel, you come and sit beside him here," she said. "Keep him talking, all right? Try to find out if he is hurt anywhere else."

Mabel nodded and sat next to her youngest son, putting her arm around him. "Now, my love, can you remember what Will said in his last letter?"

Ellie moved on to Anna. Jack was hovering close behind. The other girl's eyes were still unfocused and her breath was coming in shallow pants. She looked at Ellie as though she didn't recognize her, and flinched when Ellie went to take hold of her arm, which was cold and clammy to the touch.

"What's wrong with her?" Jack asked. "Has she hit her head too?

"No," Ellie said, crouching before Anna. The other girl startled backwards. "She's in shock. I've seen it with a lot of men who've been in the trenches – you probably have too – though it doesn't seem as severe as some of those cases. We need to get her calm and still so I can get the glass out of these cuts and clean them."

"Shell shock? But I thought that was caused by something physically damaging the nerves?"

"I'm not sure. I don't think anyone can really explain it yet. But I know what has helped in my experience. Can you get me some of that boiled water, please, Jack?"

Ellie took Anna's hands carefully in her own. They were shaking. "Anna, it's Ellie. You're going to be absolutely fine." She racked her brains for something to talk about that might get through to Anna; she could tell that at the moment the other girl wasn't even hearing her. "Anna," she said, as Jack returned with a bowl of boiled water. "Do you remember when I was rude about your family and you came all the way down to the school to give me what-for?"

Anna turned her head slowly towards Ellie, though her gaze remained blank.

"What are you reminding her of that for?" Jack asked, aghast.

"I've got to get through to her somehow. Jack, can you get my tweezers from my bag and put them in the water?"

Again, he was quick to obey, though he threw her dubious glances as he did so.

"What about the time we hadn't paid our tab at the store, and you gave me a dressing-down in front of all the other customers?"

"Ellie. . ."

"Sssh, Jack. I'll tell you something, Anna Scott, you've never been shy about letting me know when I wasn't behaving my best. And you've always been right about it. Every time. You might just be the toughest girl I've ever met."

Anna was just staring at her.

"In fact, I bet I can guess exactly what happened when that bomb went off." She felt Anna's hands tense beneath her own. "I bet I know exactly what you did. Almost all your cuts are on your arms and hands. You were trying to protect George from the glass, weren't you?"

Jack was crouched beside her now, silent in the hubbub that surrounded them.

"That was it, wasn't it? And you know what? You did it. He's got a bump on his head, but I've checked him all over and there's not one scrap of glass on him."

Anna went to speak but her voice came out in a dusty croak. She coughed and tried again through chattering teeth. "S-silly t-t-tyke was up a s-s-tep ladder w-w-when it h-h-happened. T-told him to g-g-get d-d-down. Then he f-fell w-w-with the f-first bang. H-had to c-c-cover him. . ."

"Sounds like the kind of thing he'd do," Jack said, his voice oddly husky.

"It's hard work being a big sister, isn't it?" Ellie said, smiling at Anna and reaching for the bowl with the tweezers in. "I think it might be harder than anything else I do. All right, Jack, can you get a brush from my bag and go through Anna's hair to make sure all the glass is gone."

Jack hopped up next to his sister on the pew, brush in hand. "Bet you never thought you'd see the day I brushed your hair, eh, Annie?"

Anna managed a shaky laugh. Ellie had a sudden memory of her mother brushing her own hair when she was small. It had been the nicest feeling. She wondered how old she had been when that had stopped.

As Jack pulled his sister's hair out of its dishevelled braid and began to gently tug the brush through it, Ellie lifted Anna's left arm a little, towards the light that was streaming through the high windows of the church.

Anna hissed with pain as Ellie began to carefully extract the fragments of glass from her arm, but she didn't complain. Jack and Ellie kept up a steady stream of conversation to distract her. Jack talked about his work at the new munitions factory, and Ellie told them about the hospital; all the stories, she realized, that hadn't been making it into letters to Jack for some months now.

When she explained about the prank they had been playing on Sister Adam the day that Jack had come to visit, she had to wait for Anna to stop chuckling so that she could extract the tiny shard of glass from her cheek and clean the wound.

"So, as I'm sure you can imagine, I've been Top Bedpan Collector ever since."

Anna laughed again, and Ellie glanced at Jack. He was shaking his head, but he was also smiling.

At last, she was finished. All the glass had been removed, and Anna's cuts had been cleaned and dressed.

"The best thing you can do now is get some rest. Do you want to go home? Jack could take you."

"It's all right. I'll w-wait with Mam until she and G-georgie are ready to go."

"All right, but you should lie down," Ellie told her firmly.

Anna stretched herself along the pew and Ellie pulled one of the blankets that Jack had found over her.

"Come on, Jack. It looks as though John from the Dog and Duck and Mrs Anderson from the WI are making teas. Let's bring some over to your family, and then I'll see what Aunt Frances needs me to do next."

As they walked over to the trestle table Mrs Anderson had set up, she said softly, "What happened, Jack? How could this have happened? And what happened to . . . to Sarah?"

Jack ran his hands over his face before replying. "Well, I wasn't here, as you know, and it's been hard to get a clear idea from anyone. Seems as though one of those Zeppelins suddenly appeared over the village this afternoon. You know, it happens more and more; they're usually on their way to London, or one of the other big cities. I expect this one was too, really. . . There were a few more bombs, elsewhere in the area; some fell in the harbour. The Germans probably couldn't tell what they are bombing, from that height. It was all a horrible mistake. . ."

"It was just the one bomb that hit the village, then?"

"Yes."

"And it fell on the shop?"

"Just outside at the front; that's why all the glass was shattered. Mam was out in the store cupboard at the back. Anna was working at the front and Georgie was with her. Sarah . . . Sarah was just on her way out after doing some shopping."

They stopped in front of the trestle table, and Jack poured them both tea. Ellie wrapped her hands around the cup and held it to her face, letting the steam bathe her sore eyes. "Poor Thomas," she murmured. "The poor Mertens. . ."

Jack just nodded. There was nothing else to say.

TWELVE

A DAY LATER

It was late in the evening and Ellie was just finishing some stitches on Mrs Franklin's forearm, closing up a particularly deep cut from the glass that had shattered.

"There we are," she said, cutting the end of the thread. "Well done, you were very brave."

"Tosh," said the matronly Mrs Franklin. "Once you've given birth to a child, you'll see that this pain is nothing to what—" She broke off, blushing at her boldness in speaking about such an unladylike topic.

Ellie ducked her head hurriedly into her bag of supplies so that Mrs Franklin wouldn't see her smile.

She wondered how the older woman would react if she heard the way Grace and some of the other nurses spoke. It was hard to remain prim and proper when exposed to the sorts of things the nurses were on a daily basis.

"Besides," Mrs Franklin went on, recovering herself quickly, "you were so quick and gentle; I scarcely felt anything."

Ellie beamed and opened her mouth to reply, before a sound from behind interrupted her.

"Ellie?"

The voice was soft but something about it made Ellie turn round suddenly.

Her mother stood there, so pale and insubstantial-looking that she could almost have been mistaken for a ghost. A sleepy Charlie clasped her hand, his face brightening at the sight of his sister.

"Lellie!"

"Mother!" Ellie said with a gasp as Charlie broke free and wrapped himself around her legs. "Charlie!"

Mother stepped closer and, to Ellie's great surprise, opened her arms. Ellie stepped into them, still with Charlie attached, and was embraced by her mother's bird-like frame.

"Mother, I was so worried when I heard—"

"It's so awful, so awful. . ."

Mother rested her head against Ellie's shoulder, and Ellie noticed again how much smaller her mother seemed to have become. Or was it her becoming taller? She felt dampness soaking into the sleeve of her dress.

"Don't cry, Mother. . ."

"It was so frightening. . . And, Ellie, Sarah. . ."

"I know, I know," Ellie said soothingly. "It's terrible."

"I just can't believe it. Such a sweet girl. And she's been such a help to me while you've been gone."

Ellie couldn't remember a time her mother had spoken so many words together; had volunteered so much of her own feelings. She ran her hand up and down her back, able to feel the ribs beneath her mother's dress.

"I heard you were here," Mother said, her voice muffled. "I had to see you. . ."

"Of course you did," came Aunt Frances's business-like tones as Ellie felt her own tongue grow heavy in her throat.

"Hello, Josephine," said Frances, leaning over to drop a kiss on her sister-in-law's cheek. "Hello, you," she said to Charlie, swinging him up into her arms and blowing raspberries on his neck until he squealed. "We're so glad you're safe."

"Bang," explained Charlie, solemnly. Mother nodded, but seemed to have exhausted her stores of conversation. Frances stroked Charlie's hair.

"Might I say, Mrs Phillips," Mrs Franklin chimed in, "your daughter is an absolute credit to you. An absolute credit. She has been working like a Trojan for hours, with the stamina and skill of a much older person. Isn't that right, Miss Phillips?"

Ellie was grateful that Aunt Frances took "Miss Phillips" to mean herself; she wouldn't have known what to say. She didn't dare glance at Mother; she would hate her to think her daughter was becoming prideful. And thank goodness Matron wasn't here to hear such praise!

"It certainly is," Frances said with a smile in Ellie's direction. "I'm so proud of her every day in the Brighton hospital."

Ellie's skin burned even hotter at the thought of

all the times when she knew this hadn't been the case.

"Ellie," Frances said now, "you should go home with these two and get some rest. We've done as much as we can for tonight."

"And you," Ellie urged.

"I think I'll stay here tonight," Frances replied, then held her hand up as though to ward off Ellie's protests. "We'll send the walking wounded home, but someone should stay to keep an eye on the likes of George Scott, and for when those ambulances finally get here. No need for both of us to, and besides, I have to get back to Brighton tomorrow morning on the first train – it makes sense for me to stay close to the station."

"Oh. But shouldn't I. . ."

"I'll speak with Matron when I get back, but I'm sure she'd agree that you are needed here, given that the two doctors have more than enough to contend with. At least until the ambulances can get the more serious casualties to hospital."

"Come along, Ellie." Mother's soft voice took Ellie by surprise again. "Frances is right. You need to rest if you are to be of use to people tomorrow."

Ellie stared at her for a long moment before collecting herself. "All right," she said.

Ellie slept fitfully that night. Half-dreams – of swarms of Zeppelins snarling over Endstone; the faces of the people she loved; scenes of horror interspersed with imagined conversations with Jack on the Endstone clifftops, with Sanjay in the hospital gardens – were so real they felt like memories.

When she woke, it took her a moment to remember where she was. She felt like a different person from the girl who had last slept in this bed. She sat up with a start – she had to get back to the church! – just as her mother walked in carrying a tray.

"Good morning," Mother said. "I've brought you tea."

Ellie found herself momentarily at a loss for words. She didn't think Mother had ever brought her tea in bed in all her life.

"Thank you," she said at last.

"And there's breakfast downstairs, if you've had enough sleep."

"Thank you," Ellie said again, "but I need to get back to the church. What time is it?"

"It's seven o'clock. You must eat first, Eleanor," her mother said, a hint of her usual tone creeping back in. "That is not open for debate."

Ellie smiled.

As Ellie reached the church an hour later, she saw a dark-green ambulance parked outside. Frances was supervising as young George Scott was loaded on to it. Mabel was going with him to the hospital in Canterbury.

"I'd just like a doctor to have a look at him," Frances said to Ellie. "He's woken up properly, but he was complaining of a bad headache, and was much quieter than usual."

"That wouldn't be hard," Ellie said, with an attempt at a smile.

The ambulance sputtered to life and they waved to Mabel through the back windows. "George was the only one I was worried about sending home," Frances said over the roar of the engine. "Everyone else has gone."

169

"Anna Scott too?"

"Yes, Jack took her back. She was looking a lot better. But you should check in on them all later if you can. Here, I've made a list."

Ellie took it from her. "Thank you."

"Why don't you start with Anna?" Frances said with a soft smile.

Ellie nodded and gave her a wobbly smile back.

"I have to go now if I'm to catch my train. See if you can call the hospital from the surgery later, just to update us."

"I will."

The two Phillips nurses set off across the square together. At the point where Frances must go right for the station and Ellie left for the Scotts' house, they stopped once more and embraced.

"You've done good work, Ellie. I know it may feel like a drop in the ocean compared to what the people here have suffered, but think how much worse it would have been if we hadn't come. You should feel proud." She gave Ellie a kiss on the cheek, and they went their separate ways.

As she passed, Ellie stared with grim fascination at

the bomb site. It made the familiar village square look so different, like a new scar on a well-loved face.

She hurried on, to the roads on the other side. These too were different from usual: no children played in the street, no women were hanging up washing – in fact, there wasn't another person to be seen.

At last, she reached the front door of the Scotts' tiny house. She knocked, and then pushed it open without waiting for a reply. Here again, the quiet felt unnatural. This once bustling household was so depleted, with Jack's father in prison, his older brother fighting in France, and now his mother and George at the hospital in Canterbury.

"Hello?" she called.

"Up here," came the reply.

Ellie made her way up the narrow staircase to the room that the boys normally slept in. Anna was propped up on one of the beds, looking a much better colour than she had the day before, if rather still and listless. A glance at Jack, who was perched on the end of the bed, told Ellie that he hadn't slept at all.

"Good morning, Scotts," she said, trying to sound bright and cheerful. "I saw your mother and little

George heading off to the hospital. They'll have him patched up and good as new in no time."

"You should know, Nurse Phillips," Jack said, his mouth twitching in what might have been a smile.

"How are you feeling today, Anna?" Ellie asked.

"Rotten," the other girl replied quietly, "but I'll mend."

"I should have a look at your stitches and dressings."

"Now, look here," Anna snapped, sounding for a moment just like her normal self. "I don't need the two of you sitting here watching me all day. It's bad enough just Jack moping around. I'm sure you're dying to have some time alone together and talk. Jack needs some fresh air and something to eat. And *I'd* like a bit of peace."

Ellie couldn't help it; she grinned. "Well, Anna Scott, I'm delighted to hear you're coming back to your full strength. I do need to have a proper look at you, but how about I take Jack downstairs and make him some tea first? You could try for a bit of a doze in the meantime."

Anna gave a grunt which Ellie decided to interpret as agreement, so she took Jack by the elbow and gently ushered him down the stairs.

"Not even the might of the German army can suppress that one for long," Jack grumbled.

"I heard that!" came the voice from the bedroom.

In the kitchen, Ellie pushed Jack firmly into a chair before he could make for the kettle; instead she picked it up herself and set it on the stove. When she turned round, he had his head in his hands.

"Jack?" she ventured.

He made no reply, but to her astonishment, she saw his shoulders heave.

"Jack," she said again, hurrying to his side. She pulled up a chair beside him and wrapped her hands around his arm. "Come on, Jack, talk to me. Look at me."

Slowly, he allowed his hands to be pulled away from his face. His eyes were bloodshot; his nostrils flared. Ellie's heart gave a great squeeze. "Oh, Jack," she said, taking his face in her hands. "It's all right. Everything will be all right."

"Will it?" His voice cracked. "Oh, God. El, you saw him . . . it was as if I was back in the trenches . . . as if I'd been hiding from the war and it came all the way to Endstone to find me. . ."

173

"I know. I understand. It's horrible to see someone unconscious, especially someone you love. . . It looks. . . It's shocking. I can't even imagine seeing Charlie like that. . ."

Jack gave a great juddering breath and his chin turned downwards.

"But, Jack, he's going to be fine. And now he's with the doctors he'll be getting the best possible care."

"I know, I know. . . It's just . . . everything. It's too much. This war. . . It just seems to get bigger and bigger until it smothers everything. Will there be anything left when it finishes?"

Ellie didn't know what to say. It was true; she felt the same way. Instead, she pulled his head in towards her chest and held it fiercely against her. He responded by wrapping his arms around her waist and gave in to his tears. She ran her fingers through his hair, and rocked him until he started to become calmer.

After several moments, she felt rather than heard him saying something. She couldn't make out the words so she pulled herself up straighter but he stayed pressed against her. She strained her ears instead.

"I've missed you," he was saying. "I've missed you

so much, El."

The pain in her chest was a physical one. "I've missed you too," she said, and realized as she did how true this was.

"I need you, El. I think maybe that's selfish though. You're too good for me; you always have been. I've always known that one day I'd have to give you up. But . . . but now it seems that maybe the time has come, and I can't . . . I don't want to. . ."

The pain was almost unbearable. She held him tighter against it. "Jack, no. . ." she said through gritted teeth. "No. . . There's no one in the world who's better than you. I'm sorry, I'm so sorry. I don't know why I've. . . I can't explain. . . I suppose I wanted so much to make a success of my work that I . . . I just shut myself off from everything else. . . But never, ever think that you have to give me up or that I. . ." Her voice wobbled. "Please don't give up on me, Jack. . ."

Keeping one hand tangled in his curls, she brushed his cheek with the back of the other, feeling the light stubble that covered it. This was Jack. How could she have let herself become so distant from him?

She dropped her hand to his chin, and tilted it so that he was looking up at her. Leaning down, she rested her forehead against his, marvelling at the softness of his skin there in contrast to his bristly jaw.

"Please don't give up on me," she whispered again.

"I never will," he said. And then they were kissing, their tears mingling. Ellie clung to him as though frightened of what might happen if she loosened her grip.

After several moments, she felt him give a rumbling laugh. "We could run a train with the amount of steam we've generated," he said, with a grin that triggered a mirroring smile on her own face.

"Jack!" she exclaimed, making to slap him on the arm.

"Ellie!" he replied, imitating her voice but making it far shriller, while using her brandished hand as a lever to turn her body towards the stove. There, the kettle was sending out billows of steam, causing condensation to pour down the windows as it whistled angrily.

"Oh! You meant the kettle!" Ellie leapt to her feet

and seized a tea towel to lift it off the stove, feeling a bubble of laughter rising in her throat.

As the noise from the kettle died down, they heard Anna's voice drifting down the stairs.

"If you two have *quite* finished down there, I'll have my tea now!"

THIRTEEN

TWO DAYS LATER — EARLY JULY 1917

It was two days later and Ellie was finally returning to work. She had arrived into Brighton the night before on the last train, and had risen early, keen to get back to the hospital. It had been hard to leave Endstone, and harder than ever to leave Jack, but the more urgent work was here – and besides, she knew she would never again let such a vast space grow between them.

All was bustle and busyness on the ground floor of the hospital; a new shipment of injured soldiers had just arrived. It reminded Ellie of her very first day – but how different she felt now. She knew to keep out of the way of the doctors and the trained nurses; to carry on with her own work. If they needed extra help, they would call her.

Walking into the ward, her eye was drawn straight away to the difference. Sanjay was not in his bed, which had been neatly made up. He stood beside it, dressed in his uniform, packing a few last items into his bag. His back was to Ellie, but something in his posture told her that he knew she was there.

She walked up beside him. "Shipping out, Private Das?"

He turned to face her with a small smile. "That's right, Nurse Phillips."

"When are you off?" she asked, sitting down at the end of the bed.

He sat beside her. "Soon. Now, actually. I believe the truck will be here shortly to take me and a few others to the station. I'm glad you were back in time to say goodbye."

"Me too."

"How are things at home?"

"Sad. Very sad. But luckily most people are on the mend."

"That's good."

"Yes. So. . . You're back off to France." It was a statement rather than a question.

"That's right," he said, lowering his head.

"I wish you were going home instead," she said softly, leaning towards him.

"So do I," he whispered back.

"But you will, Sanjay," she said. "I'm sure of it. You've got to get back to that little brother of yours. And besides, you owe it to me to take good care of yourself after all my hard graft nursing you back to strength."

His smile broke free; as ever it changed his face like the shaft of light falling on a mountainside. "Yes, ma'am."

"Wait!" she said, remembering. "I've got something for you." She scurried off to the supply cupboard before he could reply. She reached around in the back to find something she had liberated from its proper owner some weeks ago and hidden there in readiness for this day.

She returned to his side and pressed it into his hand. He stared at the soft square of fabric in puzzlement, opening it out to reveal the neatly embroidered *P.A.*, before understanding dawned on his face.

"Sister Adam's handkerchief!" he said, his normally level tones animated with glee. "Why, you are a *devil*!"

Ellie laughed. "That's just something to remember us by. I hope you'll write to me when you can."

"Ah." He smiled at her. "I will not be forgetting you, Eleanor Phillips. You are quite unlike anyone else I have ever met."

She ducked her head, feeling suddenly as shy as she had done when they first met. "And you are unlike anyone I've ever known. So I mean it about writing!"

He laughed again. "I will, I will. Do you think I would dare disobey, even with a safe distance between us? And in the meantime, you keep up your studies, won't you? You are a fine nurse, a fine nurse."

She swallowed hard against the lump that had once more lodged itself in her throat. "I will."

"Private Das?" It was Grace, standing in the doorway, looking unhappy at having to interrupt. "I'm sorry, but the truck is here. There is a rather rude sergeant trying to make things happen faster by roaring at everyone."

"Of course," he said, shuffling off the bed and to his feet. He hefted his bag on to his shoulder and bid farewell to his fellow patients and to Grace, whose hands he squeezed in his own.

"Go and see him off," Grace whispered to Ellie. She nodded.

They walked down the stairs together, Ellie watching with pride how Sanjay walked with almost no trace of a limp now.

Outside the entrance to the hospital, the truck waited, its engine ticking over as the sergeant gave orders and the other returning soldiers boarded.

Sanjay and Ellie stood side by side for a moment. There was nothing more to say. Suddenly he turned and seized her in a tight hug. She squeezed back, and then he was gone. She missed the warmth immediately, but drew herself upright and painted a smile on her face, ready for when he reappeared at one of the windows of the truck.

He raised his hand and she lifted her own in reply. How strange to think that she would most likely never see him again. She thought of Jack; how she hoped that he would not be returning to the front line any time soon.

Ellie gave a final wave as the truck pulled off. Then she turned and walked slowly back up the steps into the hospital, where her patients were waiting for her.

Read Ellie's entire moving story...